The Wild White Pony
and Other Girl Guide Stories

Also in Armada by Robert Moss

The Challenge Book of Brownie Stories

The Wild White Pony and Other Girl Guide Stories

by Robert Moss

An Original Armada

Armada

The Wild White Pony and Other Girl Guide Stories
was first published 1976 in Armada by
William Collins Sons & Co. Ltd.,
14 St. James's Place, London SW1A 1PF.

© Robert Moss 1976

An Original Armada

Printed in Great Britain by
Love & Malcomson Ltd., Brighton Road,
Redhill, Surrey.

CONTENTS

THE WILD WHITE PONY

POLLY PREECE, Patrol Leader of the Owls, dropped quietly on all-fours and began to worm her way forward through the undergrowth. It was not easy to move soundlessly through the vegetation of this part of Wycherly Forest, especially as everything was still and the crack of a twig breaking underfoot sounded as loud as a gunshot. But Polly was a keen and experienced stalker and had become quite adept at moving silently in forest country through trying to stalk the deer that roamed the woodlands and glades near the hamlet of Crint, where she was holidaying with her uncle, aunt and cousin Linda.

She was not stalking deer at the moment—merely trying to reach the glade where she and Linda had left their cycles. The test was to get there before Linda, or, if Linda had managed to reach the spot first, to creep in without being seen by her.

Suddenly Polly froze. Through the screen of foliage ahead she had seen something white flutter.

"Linda!" she breathed. "She's got in first!"

Feeling a trifle chagrined that her cousin had managed to beat her to the rendezvous, she determined now to break even by stealing up and into the glade unobserved. Linda, of course, would be on the watch for her, all ready to let out a triumphant yell when she spotted her. Linda, a Guide like herself, had more facilities than she for perfecting herself in stalking, tracking and woodcraft in general, living right in the heart of Wycherly Forest, but Polly rather prided herself on her own skill and had hoped to beat her cousin at the particular game they were playing.

Stealthily, scarcely daring to breath, she crept forward towards the glade. The sunlight dappled the green carpet of the forest with yellow spots and stripes. The buzz and whirr of insects made fairy music in the ferns and grasses. Scarcely a breath of wind stirred in the leaves below tree-top level.

Polly reached the edge of the glade and, stealthily parting a clump of ferns, peered through the fronds. Then her mouth dropped open in sheer astonishment.

She had made a mistake in direction finding. The glade was not the one in which she and Linda had left their cycles. It was a smaller clearing, in the centre of which a shallow pool of water mirrored the silvery trunks of two or three nearby birch saplings. But what rivetted Polly's eyes was the creature drinking at the little pond.

It was a white pony, with a long shaggy mane and tail.

Polly could scarcely believe her eyes, so utterly unexpected was the sight. There were herds of wild ponies in the forest, she knew. They ran wild until the annual round-up in September, and her uncle had told her that they all belonged to someone, each owner knowing his herd by identification marks the ponies carried. But a lone white pony was something different—something uncommon and surprising.

She had no chance of examining the pony at closer quarters or for a longer time, for all at once it lifted its head and listened, its nostrils quivering as if it scented danger. Then, swiftly and suddenly, it swung round and plunged off between the birch-trees into the undergrowth.

Polly let out an exclamation of disappointment. She would dearly have liked to observe the white pony longer. Filled with curiosity, she forgot the pathfinding contest she was engaged upon with Linda and made her way, without any attempt at concealment, back to the "home" glade, which she discovered was some distance south-east of the one with the pool in it.

Linda, who had reached rendezvous only a few minutes earlier, let out a yell when she saw her coming, but Polly ran to her excitedly and told her about the white pony.

"I've never heard of a white pony in the forest," said Linda. "I say, Polly, you're not trying to make excuses for being beaten, are you?"

"Certainly not!" cried Polly indignantly.

"You're quite sure about it, I suppose—I mean you couldn't have made a mistake about it, could you? It was a pony and not a—a——"

"D'you think I don't know a pony when I see one?" demanded Polly wrathfully. "What d'you think I might have seen, then—a white deer or a cow or perhaps even the phantom horse of Wycherly Forest?"

"Keep your stripes on, old gal," grinned Linda. "If you say you saw a white pony, of course you saw a white pony. All I'm saying is that I've never heard of such a creature in the forest."

"It couldn't belong to a riding-school or anything like that, could it? No, I don't think it could, really, because it looked unkempt and wild, not a bit like an owned horse."

"We'll ask Daddy about it when we get home."

Linda's father was head gamekeeper on a big estate and knew all there was to know about the wild life of Wycherly Forest. Contrary to Linda's belief that he would cast doubts on Polly's story of a wild white pony, he showed keen interest.

"As a matter of fact, there have been reports from time to time—mostly from children—of a wild white pony in the forest. I've never actually heard of a grown-up seeing it, but children roam over the forest for flowers and berries during holidays, and one or two have told of seeing a white pony, though I don't think anybody has paid really serious attention to it, children rather being given to imagining things or mistaking something quite ordinary for something fitting better into their land of make-believe."

"What I saw wasn't make-believe," Polly asserted.

"No, I'm not doubting the existence of this white pony now you've seen it—and at close-quarters too," said Mr. Leach thoughtfully. "I'm just wondering now whether it isn't an offspring of a cross-breeding experiment that the previous owner of the estate on which I work carried out. His object was to cross our forest ponies with Arab stock he shipped from abroad. But something went wrong with his finances, and the whole scheme tumbled about his ears. All the same, though, it is on the cards that this white pony is half an Arab, especially as there were a number of white mares among the Arab stock."

"And who would the white pony belong to, Uncle Dick, if it were caught?" inquired Polly eagerly. All her life she had longed for a pony of her own. An hour or so a week on a riding-school pony was the nearest she had come to achieving her cherished ambition.

"Sorry, Polly, but you haven't got a hope!" replied her uncle, grinning. "There's no doubt at all of the ownership. It belongs to Colonel Llewellyn, my boss, who not only took over the estate from the horse-breeding owner, but shouldered the debts as well—and the assets. Still, I'll tell him about it; he'll be interested, although just now we're both much more concerned with the deer-stealing."

Polly heard about the raiders from the big towns who had recently descended by night on the forest, killing deer with guns fitted with special silencers. The raids had caused great anger among the local folk. So vast and sparsely populated was the area of forest land, which had once been a royal hunting chase, that it was a simple matter for raiders in cars or vans to make sorties at various points of the forest, bag half a dozen or more deer, and be half-way to a big centre of population before anyone was even aware that there had been a raid. Police, gamekeepers and farmers kept watch at night in the hope of catching the raiders at their deadly work, but so far without coming within striking distance of them.

"But we hope to catch them sooner or later," said Mr. Leach grimly. "We've organised vigilante groups, each watching a section of the forest. We've arranged a code of signals by whistle, so that if raiders are spotted in one part our man there blows his whistle and the rest of us know by the number of blasts which corner of the forest it's coming from. We can only muster enough men to have one in each section, though."

That afternoon the two girls changed into Guide uniforms. Linda belonged to the 1st Glaisher Company, and Polly had been invited to join in all her Patrol activities during her stay. Glaisher was the nearest market-town, though some distance from Crint. The two Guides cycled off early, as Mrs. Leach wanted them to buy a clothes-line and pegs and various other household articles for her.

The Guide meeting was an enjoyable. one, and afterwards both girls were invited home by Linda's P.L. As they stayed to supper, it was getting late when they set off back to Crint. Their route lay through the forest, along a grassy track that provided a short cut to the hamlet.

"Isn't this thrilling?" exclaimed Polly, gazing over the great expanse of forest lying silent under the moon and stars. "I wouldn't miss it for worlds!"

The vast tracts of treeland were broken by undulating heath knee-deep in heather and bracken. Streams and pools were few in the forest, but here and there, as Mr. Leach had warned Polly when she first came, deep, treacherous bogs stretched green and inviting between the woodlands, deadly traps for unwary feet, despite being marked by DANGER notices.

"I say, Linda," said Polly presently, "I've got a great idea. How about going to the pool again? It isn't far from here, is it? That white pony might be there, you know. It might be his regular drinking-place."

"Well, we are quite near the pool, as a matter of fact," said Linda. "Father is out all night with the vigilantes, watching for raiders, but mother will get anxious if we're very late, though she thinks we're quite a responsible pair! But we mustn't be too late."

"Agreed! You'd better lead the way," said Polly. "You know the forest better than I do."

Linda turned off the grassy track a few minutes later and rode along a winding narrow path between fern-clad banks.

"We can't go much farther on our bikes," she told Polly, stopping presently. "We're better leave them here and go the rest of the way on foot."

They switched off their cycle lamps and leant their bikes against a tree. About to set off towards the pool, however, Polly clutched Linda's arm. "What's that?" she breathed. "Did you hear something?"

"No!"

"I did—a whistle."

"A whistle? Are you sure—yes, there it is!"

From somewhere far distant, but clear through the still night air, there came the long-drawn-out skirl of a whistle.

"That means deer-raiders, doesn't it?" inquired Polly grimly.

Linda nodded. "In the north-east section, as the whistle sounded only one blast. We're in the south-west—three long blasts! I'm thankful they're not in our corner! All the same, it's a bit scaring, isn't it, to feel that there are raiders about in the forest at all?"

Polly agreed. "Let's hope the vigilantes catch 'em!"

Chilled now with a sense of foreboding, the two moved quietly forward until they saw the little pool glinting in the moonlight through the undergrowth.

"Let's lie low here for a bit," whispered Polly, and,

13

creeping forward, sank down into a clump of high ferns. Linda dropped down beside her.

"I do hope the white pony comes!" she whispered.

But it seemed that their vigil was to be fruitless. For more than an hour they lay in wait without seeing so much as a deer. At last Linda yawned and stirred.

"Enough's enough," she murmured. "I vote we trek——"

Polly gripped her suddenly. "Sh! I believe there's something coming now! Yes, I'm sure of it!"

The girls held their breath. Nothing happened for a minute or two, then into the glade stepped three dim shapes. The surrounding trees screened off the moonlight, and the girls could only just see that the newcomers were deer. Even so, it was fascinating to watch the beautiful animals at close quarters as they drank at the pool.

They seemed in no hurry to go, but suddenly the girls saw all three lift their heads and listen; then, with one accord, they turned and bounded away into the undergrowth.

"Now, what's scared them——?" began Polly, but stopped as Linda clutched her arm and pointed.

Through the gap in the silver birch trees nearly opposite them, treading almost as lightly as the deer had done, appeared the white pony.

It stood for an instant, looking and listening; then, evidently satisfied that it was safe to drink, it crossed to the pool and lowered its head to the limpid water.

Polly and Linda watched, delighted and breathless. But only a few minutes passed when again there came a rude interruption. A curious noise, almost like the sound of air escaping from a burst tyre, rushed momentarily through the hush of the night. Then came a long-drawn-out cry, like that of a stricken animal. It chilled the blood of the two girls, but they had no time to wonder what it was, for the next moment the undergrowth became alive with fleeing deer. Three, four, five of them came bounding frantically from the dimness of the vegetation into the glade. Again the curious explosive sound burst out, and the hindmost deer fell, letting out a quivering cry.

The white pony had turned as soon as the deer sprang into the clearing. It raced at once for the gap between the silver birches through which it had come, but suddenly it veered away, and a moment later the two girls saw why. A man carrying a gun burst through the gap between the birches.

"Heh, Joe, quick!" he called urgently. "A white hoss! Get 'im!"

The girls had a vague impression of a second man emerging into the glade from the direction the deer had run. The white pony, alarmed, trapped on two sides, gave a loud neigh and suddenly charged towards where they were crouching. Instinctively the girls ducked. Fortunately, the pony did not keep a straight course, but turned before it reached them and tore past.

"After 'im, Chuck! 'E's worth good money. We'll come back for the deer."

As he spoke, Joe leapt across the glade and started off through the undergrowth in pursuit of the horse.

"That's it—keep arter 'im, Joe! Don't let 'im turn. I'll go this way an' head 'im off. He can't cross the Oakwood Bog. So we've got 'im!"

While Joe crashed on through the vegetation, Chuck

went at a run in the direction of the path by which the girls had come.

When he had gone, the girls scrambled up, thankful to have remained undiscovered.

Polly gripped Linda's arm fiercely. "What did they mean—he can't get away? They mustn't catch that horse, Linda! I can't bear to think of it being trapped."

"If they corner it by the bog it can't escape." Linda's voice was low and anxious. "Whatever can we do? Those men are dangerous—I've heard Daddy say so. We can only go for help. We must be careful, but we've got our bikes."

"We can bring help without our bikes!" Polly's voice was excited. "Don't forget that I've got a whistle."

"A whistle?"

"If I blow three blasts on a whistle, it will tell the vigilantes there are raiders in the south-west section. Won't it?" Polly faced her chum eagerly. "You remember that single blast we heard on the way here? Perhaps it wasn't a genuine alarm—just a decoy. Suppose it has taken the vigilante away from this section, leaving the way clear for these raiders? The answer to that is to bring him back—plus others!"

"It's a wonderful idea!" breathed Linda. "But it's terribly risky, Polly. It might bring those men on to us—first."

Polly took the whistle from her belt. "It's a risk we must take——" But Linda caught her wrist.

"Wait! Let's get to our bikes first. Then we can signal the alarm and bolt!"

16

"Fair enough." Polly nodded approvingly. "I'm sure your Guider would approve of that idea, Linda. Let's go!"

They ran. Their cycles were as they had left them. The Guides grabbed them and mounted, and then, before pedalling off, Polly raised her whistle and let three long, clear blasts skirl over the hushed forest.

"Now ride!" breathed Linda.

They rode. Speed was out of the question on the narrow forest path, and they did not risk switching on their lamps. But they rode as fast as they dared, and presently they came out on to a more clearly de-fined track running along the fringe of the woodland. But just as they turned into it, a quivering, shudder-some cry floated to their ears over the still night air. It was the desperate, piteous cry of an animal in dis-tress. It was vibrant with fear, and it stabbed a chill into both girls, who braked together.

"W-what was it?" whispered Linda. "It sounded like a stricken animal."

"I'll tell you what it was." Polly gripped her chum's handlebars fiercely and stared into her face. "It was our horse! I know it was—I feel it! Those men have got him! We've got to rescue him, Linda—we must! We can't leave him to their mercy—we *can't!*"

Linda nodded, without speaking. Her instinct was towards caution, but her sympathies for the trapped horse were as closely engaged as were Polly's.

"It may have been a deer, but whatever it was, for goodness' sake be careful! Those raiders will have got a lorry or a van hidden away somewhere. Watch your step!"

Polly nodded. Then: "Come on!" She pushed her

cycle off with one foot and pedalled furiously in the direction from which the cry had come.

But she was not beset by the fear that was beginning to grip Linda, riding close behind her, as they drew near the end of the wooded tract. She was still much of a stranger in the forest, whereas Linda knew this part of it intimately. It was not until the track made a sharp curve round a belt of trees that Linda voiced her fear with a sudden warning.

"Be careful, Polly! Slow down! We're coming to Oakwood Bog."

At that moment they swept past the last few trees, and Polly looked out over a flat expanse of lawn-like ground devoid of trees or vegetation and shimmering, almost like a breathing thing, in the moonlight.

"This is Oakwood Bog," said Linda, and then stopped, her cheeks whitening.

With a finger that shook, Polly pointed over the bog, where a white shape was clearly visible in the moonlight—struggling helplessly—hopelessly—to fight its way out of the deceptive, sinister morass into which it had ploughed in its maddened flight from the hunters.

"Our horse!" breathed Polly. "It's caught in the bog!"

Linda shook herself free from the paralysis that was gripping her. From the wood to the left she could hear the sound of receding feet. She guessed now that the two men who had hunted the wild pony to its death had given up their attempt to capture it and left it to its fate while they went back to retrieve the slain deer. Without aid, the pony was doomed.

Both girls realised that as the terrified animal let out shrill, heartrending screams.

"We've got to do something——" began Polly, almost sobbing.

"But what? No, no, we can't do anything. There's only a track along the edge of the bog——"

"The rope!" Polly turned on her swiftly. "That clothes-line—you remember, we bought one for your mother at Glaisher! It was best-quality nylon——" She dived a hand into her bicycle basket, where several of the household articles they had bought for Mrs. Leach had been put. "It might hold if we could get it round the horse. You say there's a track over the bog—where is it?"

"It's marked by white stones—look, you can just see the patches of white—but what are you going to do, Polly—what can you do?"

Polly jumped on her bike. "I don't know—yet. But come on! There may be some way of getting to him!"

Linda followed swiftly as Polly pedalled madly off. She overtook her chum and called out: "The track runs along the line of that row of big oaks—but look, Polly—the horse is yards away from the track. We'd never reach him, and even if we did——"

"I've got an idea!" Polly jumped from her bike and leant it against a tree, the first of the row of great oaks whose gnarled limbs overhung the edge of the bog. "If we could find some branches, we could lay a sort of raft across the bog to the horse that might bear my weight. I'm very light. Come on—quick, quick!"

Linda didn't stop to raise doubts. It was obvious

that the horse was in desperate straits. Its frantic efforts to break free of the terrible ooze that was slowly sucking it down only sank it lower. The slime was already over its knees, and the poor creature was sending out piteous cries of distress. Unless the girls could pull it clear it was inevitably doomed.

Both Guides grabbed up branches madly, heedless of their uniforms. There were plenty on the ground beneath the oaks, some of them with foliage. With their arms full, they ran towards the white stones that marked the track along the edge of the bog. Linda, who had been across the bog by the track before, led the way. At the point nearest to the trapped horse, she stopped and laid the largest of her branches over the surface of the bog, then others crossways on top. Polly added hers. They worked with furious energy and speed. Then, when they had placed branches as far out as they could reach, Polly turned to Linda.

"This is where the real test begins," she said grimly. "I'm going to stretch out on the branches and lay another lot at the end of these until I can reach the horse. I'm not much more than half your weight, Linda, so it's got to be me. There's no risk, really —at least, not much—not if you rope me round the waist and stand ready to pull me back if the branches don't bear my weight."

Linda nodded. "I won't let you go," she promised grimly. She took the clothes-line that Polly had brought from her bicycle basket and knotted it round her chum's waist in a competent bowline.

"Listen," said Polly. "If I can eventually get to the horse I shall have to untie the rope from myself and get it round him—somehow. But there won't be any more danger to me, because I shall still be able to hang on to the rope, which will be stretched from him to you. Mind *you* hang on to it, Linda, like grim death."

"I will," Linda promised tensely.

Polly knelt down and then with infinite care slowly wormed herself out over the raft of branches, spreading her weight as much as possible. The branch bridge moved, and an ominous gurgling noise sounded below it, but if it sank appreciably it did not submerge the top layers that the Guides had piled on above the foundation branches. Dauntlessly, inch by inch, Polly moved herself along it.

She reached the end of the bridge. Now, while still lying flat, she set herself to lay a further section with the unused branches and limbs she and Linda had tossed there in readiness. It was slow and difficult work in her cramped and dangerous position. At last, however, she had piled up enough. She called back to Linda: "Let out more rope. I think I can reach him this time."

Tentatively, as Linda paid out rope, she trusted herself on to the new section of branches. She moved forward scarcely more than an inch at a time. The horse, who seemed to have ceased its struggles and its appealing screams from sheer exhaustion, began to whinny feebly as if sensing that Polly was coming to its aid. Polly herself was too strained to speak to it; every nerve was taut as she wormed forward.

At last she was near enough to touch the horse. Slowly, taking infinite care not to make any movement likely to depress the shaky bridge into the waterlogged mass below, she unknotted the rope from her waist and reached forward to pass it round the horse. At her touch the animal shuddered, and instantly the swamp heaved and swelled, forcing Polly's heart into her mouth, and causing the branches to move like a light boat on a wave.

Polly waited until the quicksilver surface of the bog had become still again, then, murmuring soothingly to the horse, she passed the rope over its back, then reached forward under its belly and caught the end. She realised with horror that the horse's flesh was partially below the surface of the bog! It was slowly, surely, sinking—more deeply every minute.

She pulled the rope through the mud towards her. "Got it!" she breathed. "Now for a knot that'll hold —bowline?—yes, bowline!"

Never had she been more thankful for her Guide training and practice with knots. She had no fear that her knot would break loose; her one fear now was for the rope. Would it stand the strain of the horse's weight? To stop the rope biting into the pony's flesh, she thrust two short, thick branches under the rope.

"I'm coming back, Linda!" she called out. "Keep the rope taut so I can hold on to it."

The horse whinnied as she began to manœuvre back across the crazy shifting bridge, and Polly was sure that the feel of the rope about it, and her own presence, had lessened its terror and given it new hope.

The journey back was almost as terrible as the outward. Polly was nearly all in. But at last she managed to crawl back on to the welcome, safe, hard surface of the track, where she lay for a moment exhausted. She knew now that the combined strength of Linda and herself would never be equal to the task of hauling the horse from the tenacious clutch of the bog—even if the rope would bear the strain.

"We'll never do it, Linda," she murmured despairingly, raising herself up. "Our only hope is to bring help. I'm going to blow my whistle again."

"I'll blow," said Linda. "You look about whacked. I've got a lot more puff than you have, I should say."

Taking Polly's whistle she blew three long, strong blasts on it.

"If that doesn't bring help soon, I don't think we're going to be able to hold that horse up. He's going lower, and I can't hold him. Our only chance is——"

"Listen!" Polly interrupted her suddenly. "I've got an idea!" She struggled to her feet and picked up some of the slack of the rope from the ground by Linda, who was still bending all her weight on the five or six yards of rope that stretched out to the white outline of the horse. "Look, Linda—there's plenty of rope. If we threw it over one of the boughs of that nearest tree, we could get a lot more leverage on it. I've done rope-throwing at camp, and I'm fairly good at it. We'd at least be able to keep the horse from sinking any further, even if we couldn't lift it right out—and I don't think we ought to risk trying that, because I don't believe the rope would stand it."

"Good for you! That's trumps!" approved Linda. "I know now why you're a Patrol Leader, Polly. Can you hold on to the rope for a minute while I try and toss the slack over the bough?"

"Tie a good, heavy lump of wood to the end" urged Polly.

"Okay, P.L."

As soon as Polly took the rope from Linda she knew that it would be touch-and-go whether they would succeed in keeping the trapped horse above the surface of the deadly, relentless bog. The weight on the rope was such that she would not be able to withstand the pressure unaided. But when Linda, at her third attempt, got the end of the rope over the bough and they both began to haul on it, the situation changed. The leverage provided by the bough enabled them, with their combined pulling power, to feel certain of being able to keep the horse at least from sinking further into the mire. In fact, both girls were certain that they had lifted the animal slightly. But they did not attempt to do more than keep the pony up, for further strain on the rope might cause it to snap—and then all hope of rescue would be gone.

Pluckily, patiently, tenaciously, they hung on the rope, while half an hour passed, then another half, then another twenty minutes—and then, suddenly, Linda let out a shout: "Daddy! Daddy!" she yelled. "This way—quick! We're here—by the track over the bog!"

"Great Scott!" Mr. Leach gave a shout that brought two other men into view on the edge of the bog in quick time. "What's happening, Linda?"

In a very few minutes Linda was able to enlighten him. Thankfully the girls relinquished the rope to the men.

"My goodness, I've never heard of anything like this!" exclaimed Mr. Leach. "You've got a wild horse on the end of a rope! We heard your whistle signal, and came at once, but of course it takes the deuce of a time to get across miles of forest. We thought there were raiders here."

"So there were," said Linda grimly. "We'll tell you about them later. The first thing is to get the horse out."

It took close on two hours to release the wild white pony from the clutches of the bog and bring it to safety. Like the two girls, Mr. Leach would not risk the single rope's snapping, and feared also that strong pulls on it might cut painfully into the horse's flesh where it was not protected by the branches. So he sent for planks, rescue-harness and ropes from the nearest village, and so it was long past midnight before Polly and Linda, who insisted on staying to see the rescue completed, reached home. But they went to bed satisfied and happy, despite being utterly exhausted physically and emotionally.

"I'm sorry we arrived too late to catch the deer-killers," said Mr. Leach late next morning, when the two girls came downstairs after a long sleep, "but I believe the description you gave of them, Linda and Polly, will put the police on the right road to catching them. I phoned through and gave the police your sketch of them and told them they were called Joe and Chuck. The police seemed to wake up when they heard their names, and I fancy they knew them, although they wouldn't let on that they did."

Mr. Leach's prediction proved correct. Joe and Chuck were picked up and charged within the week. Although they were by no means the only raiders of deer, they were the first to be caught, and the police believed that the sentence they were likely to get would prove a severe deterrent to others with designs on the forest creatures.

It was wonderful news to Mr. Leach, who had worked under great strain and worry for weeks.

"Now I've got some good news for you," he told the girls. "Colonel Llewellyn confirmed what I said—that the wild white pony is his by legal right, but he insists that by right of discovery and rescue he's yours. I'm sure nobody would disagree with that."

"Ours?" cried Polly. "Surely you don't mean——?"

Mr. Leach smiled. "I do mean it—and so does the Colonel. He's making the horse over to you just as soon as it's broken in and fit to ride, and he's coming to see you both to thank you personally for what you did the other night. He's immensely impressed, I can tell you. He says that if that's what Girl Guide training does for girls he'll do something about providing a really good camp site for them on his estate in the forest."

"Why—why——" breathed Polly, "this is wonderful—isn't it, Linda?"

"Even more for me than for you, really," laughed Linda. "I imagine the pony will be kept here, and you'll only be here at holiday times, whereas I shall have the use of him all the time. What d'you say to that?"

"I don't mind that a bit." Polly sighed happily. "I'm thrilled to bits at the thought of having a pony of my own—even more at sharing him with you, Linda. Sharing him is twice the pleasure. Now we've got to think of a name for him. What do you suggest, Linda?"

"How about Oakwood? No, no, that won't do! Wycherly—how does Witch sound? No, it doesn't really fit."

"I know!" cried Polly, "It was midnight when he was finally rescued. How about calling him Midnight?"

"Midnight—good!" said Mr. Leach.

"Super!" cried Linda. "It's a lovely name, Polly, just right—and somehow thrilling. Just think of our lovely wild white pony—Midnight!"

LAME BIRD OF THE ROBINS

NEVER in all her life had Pauline felt so wretched. During the whole of her last year in Brownies she had dreamed of being a Guide. Then, when at last she had grown up and donned all the glory of Guide blue, she felt the summit of her ambitions was reached. Now she was tasting the joys of camp—camp in a real tent, with out-of-doors cooking and all the thrills of the camp-fire.

Only the joy wasn't there! Somehow, right from the beginning of her entry into the Robin Patrol, things had gone wrong. She didn't quite know how or why, but in some odd, perplexing way she had started off on the wrong foot and never after that managed to fall into step with the rest of the Patrol.

But she didn't really know why? When she faced up to the situation, reluctant though she was to do it, Pauline knew that at the root of the trouble was Nancy —Patrol Leader Nancy Berens.

From the first she had failed to hit it off with Nancy. The Patrol Leader of the Robins was keen, efficient, brimful of ideas—and horribly critical. At least, that was how Pauline saw her. And Pauline, being shy, sensitive and quick to catch impressions, felt the P.L.'s disapproval when in her first nervousness she fluffed, said or did the wrong thing, or otherwise failed to reach the high standard P.L. Nancy set for the Robins.

Now, under the surface, she was sure, Nancy was antagonistic to her.

"She'll be a lot more after this afternoon," Pauline muttered miserably. "I'll be the lame bird of the Robins all right!"

The situation was certainly difficult. She was alone, separated from the rest of the Patrol—lost! Mist completely blotted out the landscape. It had lain in patches, dense here and there and then thin and wispy, affording visibility for twenty or thirty yards. And she had fallen into a pit where it was as thick as soup!

"I would drop into the thick of it!" reflected Pauline bitterly. "That's just exactly what I would do!"

The Robins had set off from camp soon after lunch on a Patrol hike. It had promised well, and even Pauline had felt her spirits rise as they climbed over the downs and then through charming downland hamlets to the sea. They had enjoyed tea in the sunshine and set off on the return route in gay spirits. Then, with disconcerting suddenness, mist had come in from the sea and hung over the smiling landscape in a blank grey distorting veil.

The Patrol had waited, hoping that the mist would lift, but finally Nancy decided that they must move. It wasn't a complete blackout, and if they could find a road they should be able to work their way slowly back to camp. So the P.L. dispatched three girls to different compass points, with a view to finding a road or a signpost. With typical efficiency she had devised a code of signals-by-shout to ensure that the three wouldn't stray out of earshot. The code was doubtless sound and equal to most contingencies—except the one that befell Pauline.

Pauline had tripped over something that felt like wire and fell sprawling. This would not have been serious, but instead of staying where she fell she went sliding irresistibly on down a steep slope covered with a loose, slippery mixture of gravel and earth. By the time she reached the bottom of the slope she was bruised, battered, breathless—and out of call of the Patrol, of whom she had since heard nothing more.

Where was she? She could only suppose she was at the bottom of a quarry or one of the deep pits that broke the smooth swell of the downs, for while on the higher ground the mist was patchy, down in the pit or quarry or whatever it was it seemed almost solid.

"Well, I'd better try to climb back up again," she murmured.

She began the ascent. She couldn't see an inch ahead, and when she slipped on the treacherous, loose surface and slithered back down for several yards her vivid imagination began to paint fearful pictures of what lay below. Suppose she hadn't landed at the bottom of the quarry, after all, but only on a kind of shelf, and that on the edge of the shelf was a dizzy drop through black space? She shuddered and resolved to stay put where she was and wait till she could see more clearly what her situation was.

She waited. Once she thought she heard distant voices, and hopefully gave the Patrol call, but there was no response to it—nothing but blank, dank silence.

Hours seemed to pass, but still the mist lay like a pall over the world. Then, far in the distance, a low, dull reverberation came to her ears. She listened intently, and concluded that it was a distant train rumbling slowly through the mist. The sound grew steadily louder, but it wasn't until the train, its carriages aglow with light and dispersing the mist alongside, came into the straight cutting below her that she realised the surprising truth. She had not fallen into a quarry or a pit. She had slithered down a steep-sided railway embankment and was sitting nearly at the bottom of a cutting through which ran a double line of railway tracks!

She sprang up. She could have cried out with relief. She was in no danger from the train, which was travelling slowly because of the mist and which had several yards of clearance from the side of the embankment. All she had to do now was to walk along the side of the track until she came to a station, which she was bound to do in time.

She ran down the few yards of slippery incline to the floor of the cutting and was about to hurry after the train when she came to a startled stop. The train had ground to a halt. Outlined now by the lights of its carriages was a wooden shed, set in a recess of the embankment. And out of the shed suddenly rushed two rough-looking youths. They looked about seventeen or eighteen. Both were hatless. One was tall, the other short and stocky.

"This way, Ned—quick!" shouted the taller of the two, and led the way in what seemed to Pauline to be an agitated scramble up the embankment.

There was no doubt that the youths were fleeing in

panic, for the tall one cast a swift, anxious glance behind as he climbed and clawed his way in desperate haste up the slippery slope. It was evident to Pauline that they had either been hiding in the shed or doing something unlawful in there. The train was moving again now, and Pauline ran towards the shed, hoping to get a glimpse inside with the aid of the train's lights before the last carriages passed it.

She just managed it. The door was wide open, and before the end carriage moved beyond it she could see that the shed was a storehouse of some kind of gangers' implements. There were boxes and pickaxes and sleepers and iron chains. That was all she saw before the train rumbled on and left her in the misty gloom. She turned away. Suddenly the mist was pierced by the light of a lantern and out of the greyness came a horny hand, which gripped her arm fiercely, triumphantly.

"Got you, by James! I thought you'd gave me the slip, but I've copped you red-handed!" Her captor turned and yelled in a loud voice: "Come on, Bill—I got one of them!"

It was then that Pauline panicked. She guessed now why the two youths had scuttled out of the shed —because they had seen the railwayman's lantern coming through the mist towards the shed. The railway linesman, or whatever he was, must have seen the youths by the light of the train, and now believed that in Pauline he had one of the trespassers. It was the realisation that she was a trespasser, although an innocent enough one, that made Pauline decide there and then to run for it. It would be too awful if she couldn't make the man believe she was not associated with the two youths and with whatever misdeeds they were committing. And she had a feeling that she wouldn't be able to!

With a sudden swift twist, she broke free of his grasp. He cursed loudly and grabbed at her again, but Pauline had already turned and now tore at top speed back along the cutting the way she had come. The railwayman pounded after her, shouting to her to stop, but the Guide raced on, gradually increasing the distance between them. She did not slow down until she saw the lights of a station dimly through the mist. Then, breathless and panting, she turned and began to climb on all-fours up the slithery side of the embankment.

She reached the top at length, where to her surprise she was able to make out with moderate clearness the outline of posts and a wire fence. Then she realised that although the mist hung thick and sticky in the deep railway cutting it was very much lighter on the higher open ground above it.

"With a bit of luck," she muttered, "I'll soon find out where I am."

She was right. Half a mile on was a signpost, which, by peering closely, she was able to read. She discovered that she was four miles from camp, and that the lane branching off at right-angles to the one she was on led to it.

Tired, dirty, subdued in spirit, she turned her weary feet along it.

She reached camp an hour and a half later—to find the remainder of the Robin Patrol in a state of anxiety over her and the Guider in process of organising search-parties to find her.

In reply to Patrol Leader Nancy's accusing "Where in the world did you get to, Pauline?" she answered flatly and uninformatively, "I got lost in the mist." And that, she determined, was all she was going to tell of her hair-raising and—she had to face it—even slightly disreputable adventure.

She slept like a log that night. Till now she had slept only fitfully at camp, waking up at intervals throughout the night—mostly with cold feet! But she was worn out and was fast asleep within minutes of crawling into her sleeping-bag.

When she did awake it was with a violent start. At first she thought it was morning, for the tent flap was open and outside was commotion and noise. But a bright moon was floating in the sky, and two girls she saw flash past her tent were in pyjamas.

She struggled out of her sleeping-bag. Above the cries that filled the air outside she distinguished the voice of a Guider, Miss Trueman, shouting orders.

A quick glance round the tent told Pauline that she and one other girl, Sheila, were the only representatives of the Robin Patrol left in it. Patrol Leader Nancy and the others had evidently gone outside.

Pauline lost no time in doing likewise.

A startling scene met her eyes. A pitched battle was being fought by Guides, led by P.L. Nancy, and two youths, whom Pauline recognised at a glance as the rough-looking couple of the railway shed. Miss Trueman, who was still in uniform, was directing operations as she struggled up from the ground.

The youths were decidedly getting the worst of it. The Guides, growing in number every minute as they rushed from all quarters, had grabbed up poles, sticks and even cooking utensils and were belabouring the two youths from three sides.

As Pauline darted out, the youths broke and fled, hotly pursued by the Guides. Miss Trueman, however, called them back.

"Let them go, girls! They've had their lesson, and they're not likely to forget it. They won't come back in a hurry."

"But what happened, Miss Trueman?" inquired P.L. Nancy. "You're hurt, aren't you?"

"Nothing to worry about—thanks to you all. I'd been to visit a friend who lives in the district and came back to camp very late," the Guider explained. "I heard a noise in the store tent. When I peeped in I saw those youths filling a sack with our food! As soon as they saw me they attacked me—quite savagely. They knocked me down. All I could do was just yell for help. I must say," she added, with a grin, "I didn't yell in vain! Thanks to you especially, Nancy, they didn't have a chance to hurt me badly; you came so quickly. There's the sack they were filling; you can see what inroads they'd have made into our larder! I'll go down to the village tomorrow and report it to the police-constable there. Now, are there any injuries among you? No? Good! Now you'd better all go back to bed—and thanks, all of you, for doing battle so swiftly and bravely!"

"And I missed it!" said Pauline disgustedly, as she walked back to the tent with the Robins' Second, Jo. "I wish one of you had woken me."

"If the row outside didn't wake you, nothing short of an earthquake would," replied Jo unfeelingly.

Back in their tents the Guides excitedly discussed the dramatic happening.

"I've known cows invade the camp," said Jo, who was a camping veteran, "and sheep, but this is the first time we've had human raiders."

"They looked a tough pair," remarked Yvonne. "I shouldn't think they're villagers."

"Has anybody come across them before, I wonder?" inquired Nancy, glancing round the tent.

"I saw them——" began Pauline unthinkingly, and then stopped. She wished heartily she hadn't spoken; she had intended saying nothing about the episode on the railway.

"You saw them—where?" asked Nancy, with interest.

"I—I don't think it was them, perhaps, after all—I mean, I'm not really sure."

"I shouldn't have thought anyone could mistake them, once seen," observed Nancy dryly. "They're the long and short of it, and both scruffy."

"It—it was foggy, so I didn't get a very clear view of them—I mean, not close up."

Nancy looked intently at her, but said nothing more, and Pauline snuggled down into her sleeping-bag to avoid further interrogation.

But her adventure in the mist was brought sharply back to mind the next day, when a burly man came to the camp and asked to see the lady in charge. Pauline's heart missed a beat when Miss Trueman called the whole company together when the visitor had gone and told them that a railway detective was investigating a theft of tools, fog detonators, and other railway property from a gangers' shed on the permanent way near Rexford Station.

"One of the men patrolling the line near the station put the silly notion into his head that Guides had something to do with it. I told him that was sheer nonsense and that Guides are neither thieves nor fools —and they'd have to be both to filch things that would be completely useless to them. I think," added the Guider, with a smile, "I've convinced him that he'll have to look elsewhere for his criminals."

That was all that was said, and Pauline was thankful for it—thankful too for Miss Trueman's blunt directness, which sometimes disconcerted people who didn't know her. She had felt the colour flood into her cheeks as the Guider was speaking, and silently prayed that no one would notice. She was guilty of nothing more serious than trespass on railway property for the sole purpose of finding her way home through the mist, and she shrank from having to confess that she'd got herself mixed up in a raid on railway stores by two young toughs. She hadn't gained standing enough in the Company or the Robin Patrol to survive revelation of such a blunder!

Camp life went smoothly and uneventfully on after this. Pauline had moments of happiness, but the barrier between her and the rest of the Patrol, real or fancied, did not break down.

"Yes, I'm the lame bird of the Robins all right," she told herself sadly.

It wasn't that the other members of the Patrol left her out of things in any way; they were friendly and jolly, but Pauline couldn't feel at one with them, and whenever she could she took herself off on solitary rambles, explaining when questioned that she was working out a challenge connected with "Enjoying the Out-of-Doors", which was a part of Guiding that deeply interested her. This was all perfectly true. The woods near the camp were a natural bird-sanctuary, and Pauline, who lived in a London suburb and saw only a few common birds, was thrilled when she noticed a woodpecker run up the trunk of a beech-tree. After that she watched the tree daily and had the joy of a close study of two great spotted wood-peckers who had made their home somewhere high up in the beech.

For the last night of camp the Guiders planned a big campfire, to which a number of visitors were in-vited. A circle of logs and benches were set up round the fire, and the Guides were to sing camp-fire songs, perform a fire-dance they had learned, and wind up with a farewell ceremony round it. The fire—a huge one—had been built on a large patch of waste ground well outside the camp site. Pauline, with the rest of the Company, spent most of the last afternoon prepar-ing for the camp-fire feast and ceremonies, but soon after tea she hurried off to enjoy a last wander through the wood, hoping too that she might get one more glimpse of her woodpeckers.

The wood was still, and greying with the coming of the dusk. The tall beech in which the woodpeckers had made their home stood on the edge of the wood. As Pauline trod softly towards it, something rustled among the leaves at its foot. She halted and watched. Then her eyes widened and she gave a gasp. The movement had been caused by a small black-and-white object with a splash of scarlet upon its head.

"Why, it's a baby woodpecker!" breathed Pauline, and darted forward. "It must have fallen out of its nest."

She picked the pretty fledgling up and examined it gently. It did not appear to have been injured by its fall, but Pauline knew that if she left it on the ground it would soon fall prey to a stoat or weasel or grass-snake or other enemy.

"I must put it back into its hole," she decided.

She had seen the woodpeckers running up the trunk of the beech, but she hadn't seen the hole in which they were likely to be living. She only hoped it wasn't too high up in the tree, because she had a poor head for heights!

Before leaving the camp she had slipped a jumper over her shirt. Now she made a soft cradle for the baby bird by turning up the bottom of the jumper and securing it with her Promise badge. Then, taking great care not to hurt the fledgling, she began to climb the tree.

It was hard work and slow work. She was handi-capped by the need for protecting the baby wood-pecker from knocks against the branches and twigs, but she climbed perseveringly on and up.

When she came out above the adjoining trees she shuddered slightly. She was much too high for her comfort! But she hadn't to climb further on up. Straight in front of her where the trunk forked rose a massive decayed limb in which a hole had been pecked. It was unmistakably the woodpeckers' nest. Thankfully, Pauline withdrew the fledgling from her jumper, holding fiercely on to a branch with her free hand. Then, leaning perilously forward, she inserted the baby bird into the hole. It uttered a queer little squawking sound, which Pauline could only hope was a thank-you or at least a grunt of satisfaction, and then disappeared inside.

"That's that," murmured Pauline—"thank goodness!"

Climbing down was likely to be easier than climbing up, but about to begin the descent she paused and listened. Footsteps were coming through the wood. Voices floated clearly up to her—and then she froze. She had heard those accents before. A glance down confirmed her suspicions. The voices belonged to the two youths she had encountered on the railway line and who had attacked Miss Trueman.

Pauline stayed where she was. She had no wish to make her presence known to the youths, who were not likely to feel kindly disposed towards Guides after their recent discomfiture by them. To Pauline's dismay, however, the two did not pass out of the wood. Close to the beech was a stile giving access to the waste ground in the middle of which the Guides' camp-fire was built, and over this the youths leaned to talk.

"Now's the time, while they're all in the camp," said the shorter of the two, whom Pauline knew to be "Ned". " 'Ow many 'ave you got, Toddy? I only got a couple."

"You don't want more'n a couple—don't want more'n one, really. But better put in two, jus' in case one turns out to be dud. Two ought to blow the blinkin' fire sky-high and 'alfway to London!"

"It'll pay them Girl Guides out proper, any'ow—an' we'll be 'ere to see it!" Ned laughed viciously.

Up the tree, Pauline listened breathlessly. It was clear from what the youths said that they were planning some kind of vengeful act against the Guide Company, but Pauline did not understand Toddy's reference to blowing the camp-fire sky-high until, looking down, she saw Ned take two small metal objects from his pocket and show them to his companion.

"Sure they'll go off in a fire?" he inquired. "On the railway they explode when a train goes over 'em, don't they?"

"They got explosives in 'em, 'aven't they?" Toddy grinned. "You just wait an' see what 'appens when the fire gets to 'em!"

Pauline gripped the tree, horrified. Now she understood! The small round objects were railway fog detonators, which she remembered the railway official had told Miss Trueman were among the articles stolen from the gangers' shed. And Ned and Toddy were going to put them—dangerous explosives—in the Guides' camp-fire!

"Thank goodness I've overheard what they're going to do?" thought Pauline.

But her satisfaction at this was short-lived. Only one of the two youths—Ned—climbed the stile and ran, stooping, towards the Guides' camp-fire. The other, Toddy, stayed by the stile, watching. Pauline dare not climb down. When Ned returned, Pauline realised, with a thrill of fear, that she was trapped indefinitely up the tree.

"Done it!" Ned announced triumphantly. "Nobody saw me. I stuck 'em both in different places."

"Good! It won't be long now, by the looks o'

things," said Toddy. "There's a lot of folks in the camp. And we'll 'ave a grandstand view from 'ere."

With something like despair, Pauline gazed across the waste ground to the camp. If she shouted, the chances were that she would be heard only by the youths below—and they would certainly make sure she gave the Guides no warning. She had nothing to signal the camp with—no flags, no matches, no flashlamp. There was nothing she could do to avert the dangerous catastrophe that threatened Guiders, Guides and spectators alike when the fire reached the detonators— unless—— Suddenly she caught her breath. The limb on which she was standing reached out widely towards the next tree, overlapping a long branch stretching from the other. If she dared, it would be possible for her, at great risk, to climb along the outstretching branch to the next tree, which stood far enough away from the youths to give her a chance of reaching the ground by it unseen by the youths.

The risk appalled Pauline, but she knew she had to take it.

As silently as she could, she climbed up and along the spreading limb. Rigid at first, it began to bend as she snaked perilously along its tapering length. She didn't dare look down, but she was conscious of the awful gulf that yawned below her. She tried to control her imagination, which told her that the limb was going to snap suddenly under her weight, that she wouldn't be able to hold on if it bent further, that she would fall in the act of trying to bridge the gap between the two trees. Once she stopped altogether while she fought to quell a sudden upsurge of sheer panic. Then, white-faced and tight-lipped, she inched on again.

She reached the end of the limb—or the point where the opposite overlapping branch looked to be most easily grasped. This was the worst moment of all. Balancing precariously, with her left hand clutching the limb, Pauline reached out with her right and grasped the other branch. Then, having secured a firm hold, she began the hair-raising task of getting herself on to it.

She never knew how she accomplished it. Oblivious of whether the youth below heard her, heedless of her clothes, of bruises, tears or scratches, she somehow managed to scramble on to the branch. She clung there for a minute, as for dear life, then, summoning all her reserves of strength antd nerve, began to worm her way towards the main trunk, which she reached after the worst five minutes of her life.

"Safe!" she breathed.

Then she looked round and down. She could just glimpse the two youths through the foliage. They were leaning over the stile, just as she had seen them when she began to climb. They had no suspicions of her presence!

Whilst she was not yet out of the wood, the worst was over. Climbing quietly down the tree was tricky in the gloom, but she succeeded in reaching the ground without attracting the attention of the youths. Then, utilising the lessons she had learned in Guide stalking and tracking games, she stole through the undergrowth to the edge of the wood, and then, drawing a deep breath, tucked her elbows into her sides—and ran.

She knew the youths would see her from whichever part of the wood she crossed the waste ground, but the one urgent, vital need was to get to Miss Trueman before she kindled the camp-fire. As she looked out from the wood she had seen the visitors gathering round the pile of the fire. Now, as she ran, she saw Miss Trueman leading a twisting crocodile of Guides from the camp to the fire—and she was brandishing a torch of fire!

"Miss Trueman, Miss Trueman!" yelled Pauline. "Stop! Don't light the fire!"

No one heard her. Desperately she spurted. Miss Trueman weaved into the camp-fire circle.

"Miss Trueman," yelled Pauline again. "Don't light the fire! It's dangerous!"

The Guider stopped suddenly. She had heard the small, agonised voice. In amazement she stared at the filthy-faced, bedraggled figure tearing frantically towards the camp-fire.

"Pauline! Pauline! Wherever have you been? Whatever do you mean——?"

"The fire will explode!" cried Pauline. "There are detontoners in it——" In her agitation she mispronounced the word. "I saw the men put them in!"

Miss Trueman handed the torch to the Assistant Guider and ran to Pauline, put her arm round her panting form, escorted her into the circle, and made her sit down.

"Now," she said, "take your time and tell us what you mean."

And Pauline did. Breathless, gasping, she poured out her story.

"I think," said Miss Trueman quietly, when she had finished, "we'll postpone our fire-kindling ceremony,

44

dismantle our fire, find the detonators, and then build it up again. We won't be robbed of our camp-fire by hooligans, however dangerous they are—and, thanks to you, Pauline, we won't be blown up, either!"

That was all she said—then. She despatched a message to the village policeman, who was able to take the youths by surprise and charge them with the theft of railway property. Then, when Pauline came back from being cleaned up and fed, she told the assembled company what the newest Robin had done—and the cheers rang very pleasantly in the ears of the "lame bird". But even more pleasant—and surprising—to Pauline were the words of Patrol Leader Nancy to her when the most exciting and memorable camp-fire ever had died down and the Company had retired to their tents for the last night of camp.

"Jolly good show, Pauline! You're a credit to the Robins—but, then, *I always knew you would be!*"

TELEVISION CAPTURE

"I'LL be at the bus-stop to meet you from Guides, Wendy," said Wendy Walker's father, who was kneeling behind the television set, doing something to the works.

"I hope you'll have fixed the TV set by then, Daddy. There's a programme I specially want to see."

"It'll be supper and bed for you as soon as you get in, you young scamp," retorted her father. "The chances are, anyhow, that the TV won't be behaving itself any better then than now. We haven't been free from interference a single night since we bought the set. I suppose it's all the cars we're getting through the village these days."

"There aren't many cars at night," said Wendy. "Perhaps washing machines and vacuum cleaners and spin-dryers and things like that cause the trouble."

"There aren't many housewives using washing machines and spin-dryers at night, either," grunted her father. "Well, you'd better pop off now, Wendy, or you'll be late for your precious Guide meeting."

Wendy had gone up to Guides only a few weeks before. She had been in the Elf Six of her Brownie Pack, but now she was a proud member of the Kingfisher Patrol of a Guide Company. The Kingfishers were the smartest Patrol in the Company, and for three years had held the shield awarded the Patrol with top points. Wendy was very proud to belong to it, but was privately rather doubtful whether she'd ever manage to be a credit to it, as she wasn't gifted like Jenny Jordan, the Patrol Leader, or Margaret Pethwick, the Second.

Bidding her father goodbye, she stepped out into the dark country lane in which their cottage stood and hurried into the village, where the bus for Millhall was waiting.

"I ain't sure the bus'll be running tonight, missy," the bus conductor told her gloomily, as she climbed in. "Some of our chaps are on strike, an' we may get word any minute not to take the bus out."

"Oh, but I've got to get to Guides," cried Wendy, in dismay, "and it's too far to walk!"

"Well, it ain't 'appened yet," the conductor told her kindly, "and if we don't 'ear something in the next few minutes we'll be off. Meself, I don't want to strike, but I got to if the rest does—see?"

Wendy nodded. She had only one concern—that was to get to the Guide hall in Millhall in time for the meeting—and she breathed a sigh of relief when the bus-driver climbed into his seat and started up the engine. She fished in the pocket of her uniform for her fare.

"Well, we'll get you there, missy, but it's a toss-up whether there'll be a bus to bring you back from Millhall tonight," said the conductor, as he punched Wendy's ticket.

"Get me there—that's the main thing," said Wendy cheerfully.

Jenny greeted her with a smile when she stepped into the Guide hall.

"Glad you were able to get here, Wendy. There was

some talk of a bus strike, and I thought you might be cut off. Our Guider hasn't come yet, but she's got a car, so it can't be the strike. Have you ever played Kim's game? No? Well, we'll see how good you are at it. It's a memory game, you know. It's fun."

Wendy proved to be quite marvellous at Kim's game. She remembered fifteen out of fifteen objects, then twenty-three out of twenty-five. The Assistant Guider, who took the meeting in the absence of the Guider, declared that Wendy was quite outstanding. Jenny was astounded.

Jenny's route home lay part of the way with Wendy's, and the two girls waited together at the bus-stop, talking—until at last Jenny realised she had been waiting very much longer than usual.

"I say, do you think the bus strike is on?" she asked Wendy "The bus ought to have been here by now."

They waited a further fifteen minutes, then Jenny grimaced. "I'm afraid it's a long walk home for us, Wendy."

"We'd better start, then," said Wendy, rather anxiously. "Dad and Mum will worry if I'm not in to time."

"I'm afraid neither of us will be."

They set off briskly. When they reached the next hamlet, Begley, Jenny had an idea.

"There's a short cut over the fields to Luscombe, Wendy, and it'll be much quicker for you to get to Selcombe than going all the way by road." Jenny lived at Luscombe, which was about a mile from Wendy's home at Selcombe.

"If you're sure you know the way, it suits me," responded Wendy.

"Over the stile, then."

The night was moonless, and presently Jenny became unsure of her direction.

"I'm not sure I haven't gone wrong."

Wendy pointed. "Lights!" she exclaimed. "They must be the lights of Luscombe."

The lights were only pinpoints winking through a curtain of trees, but the Guides hurried towards them eagerly.

"Oh, it's only a building among the trees!" said Wendy disappointedly, halting suddenly.

She was right. The lights they had thought were those of Luscombe came from a farm outbuilding or group of sheds set back some distance from the track they were following.

"We'd better ask the way to Luscombe there," said Jenny.

Wendy nodded, then stopped and held up her hand. "Listen! What's that funny noise?"

A low droning sound, almost like the murmur of an aeroplane engine, buzzed through the silence of the night.

"It may be a generator making electricity for the farmhouse," said Jenny. "Come on—let's go and see."

When they reached the building, however, which was a big barn or timber shed, they had trouble finding an entrance in the dark. Through a chink in the wall, Wendy peered in.

"It's a garage, by the look of it. There are cars in it being repaired."

Jenny squinted through the chink. "It's that electric spraying machine they're using that's making the droning noise. We'd better find the door and ask our way."

They were still searching for the door when suddenly a harsh voice behind them made them both jump.

"What are you doing here? What d'you want?"

Both girls swung round. Through the gloom they could make out the figure of a powerfully built man.

"Gosh!" exclaimed Wendy. "You did make me jump!"

"We were trying to find a door to ask the way to Luscombe," Jenny told him.

"If you're going to Luscombe what are you doing here? You're well off the road and you're trespassing. You're nearer Selcombe. Luscombe's right the other side of the woods."

"We lost our way tramping across the fields," explained Wendy.

"There wasn't a bus back from Millhall because of a strike," added Jenny.

"I see." The voice was less harsh and suspicious now. "Well, you're very near Selcombe. I'll show you the track to it."

Gladly the Guides followed the big man, who led them alongside one wall of the shed and showed them a track running along the edge of the wood. As they passed through a pool of light that filtered on to the ground from a high window they saw the big man clearly for a moment. He was wearing a boiler-suit and had a mop of hair on a bullet-shaped head.

"Luscombe is on the far side of this wood," he told them. "Off you go, and mind you don't come this way again—it's private land."

The two girls set off thankfully along the path, watched by the big man.

They reached Selcombe in quite a short time. There, Wendy invited Jenny into her house. Her elder brother, who was a Venture Scout, offered to see Jenny home after she had sat down for refreshment.

"I say, Daddy," said Wendy, after she had told the family of the evening's adventure, "do you think that electric spraying machine, or whatever it was Jenny saw, could be the thing that causes our TV trouble?"

"By George, that's an idea!" agreed her father. "You say the place isn't far away, Wendy? If the machine is a powerful one I dare say it could affect sets in the village here. I must ask somebody about it who understands the working of television."

By the time the next Guide meeting came round the bus strike was over. The Guider was at the Guide hall this time when Wendy got there.

"I couldn't get here last week," she explained to the Company. "When I went to get my car it had gone—yes, stolen! I haven't seen it since. I had to come by bus tonight. I hope to goodness the police trace it, but the chances are pretty thin now that I shall ever see it again. There's been quite a wave of car thefts all over the county. I'd be obliged if you'd all keep an eye open for it as you go about, Guides, and tell a policeman at once if you spot it."

"What is the number?" asked Linda Markham, Second of the Owls.

"The number's HUF 63 N," the Guider told her, "but it isn't likely to keep it. The first thing car thieves do is to change the number plate. They—why, is something up, Wendy?"

Wendy had put her hand up and was looking excited.

"Please," she said, "did you say HUF 63 N?"

"I did," answered the Guider, puzzled. "Why, Wendy? Have you seen it on the road since last week?"

"Yes—I mean, no—I mean, not on the road. I saw that number in the shed we looked in when we lost our way across the fields from Begley last Tuesday."

"What do you mean—you saw the number?" inquired Jenny, puzzled, turning to Wendy.

"I saw that number—HUF 63 N—on a number-plate that was standing against a wall in the shed. I remember it because I thought how funny it sounded HUF—you know, 'HUFF' and 'PUFF'."

The Guider walked over to Wendy. She was looking serious. Wendy felt rather embarrassed and was grateful when Jenny spoke up.

"Wendy and I took a wrong turning crossing the fields to Luscombe. We peeped into a big shed, because we wanted to ask our way."

"And that's where I noticed the number-plate," added Wendy.

"But what about the number?" asked the Guider. "Can you be quite sure it was 63, with HUF in front of it and N behind it?"

Wendy nodded. "Yes, I'm quite sure," she asserted.

"Wendy played Kim's game last week," put in the Assistant Guider, "and she startled us with her amazing memory. I don't think she's likely to have made a mistake over a number-plate when she got twenty-three out of twenty-five objects right at her first try."

"But whatever were you doing here, Daddy?" cried Wendy.

"What do you think? I came to see if I could stop the interference on our TV, of course! Don't you remember you said yourself that the electric spraying machine Jenny had seen in the shed might be the cause of all the trouble we've had with the TV, so tonight I thought I'd come and investigate. A car drove into the place just as I got here, and so I followed it in—and didn't come out again."

"And the car was a stolen one," said the police-sergeant, coming up. "Now, thanks to your clever Girl Guide daughter, who remembered the number on a car-plate she saw here, we've run a whole dangerous gang of car-thieves to earth. They brought stolen cars here, changed their number-plates, and disguised them with new paintwork. Last week, unluckily for them, they brought in the Girl Guide leader's car, and at the Guide meeting tonight Wendy here heard the registration number and identified it as the very one she'd seen lying on the floor of this shed last week. What d'you think of that?"

"I think it's magnificent—that's what I think," said Wendy's father. "I'll make sure Wendy gets to Guides every week after this, bus strike or not!"

"Don't forget how Jenny helped, will you, Daddy?" put in Wendy, shyly.

"Indeed I shan't," said her daddy.

"I shan't forget, either," said the Guider. "You've been the means of getting my car back, for which I'm very grateful indeed. Thank you, Wendy and Jenny."

"It was Wendy's show, really," Jenny said generously. "It was being an expert at Kim's game that did the trick." She turned to Wendy. "Margaret Pethwick said she's jolly glad you've come into the Kingfishers, Wendy. So am I!"

"So am I," said Wendy happily.

THE SWALLOWS FIRST CAMP

"SHE'S a show-off," said Brenda emphatically.

"She certainly knows we're here," agreed Anne.

Jane, the Patrol Leader, hoisted herself on to her knees and gazed speculatively at the girl on horseback on the far side of the field. "Oh, I don't know," she said. "She's jumping the pony, or training it, and I dare say that's all there is to it."

"Good old Jane; always looking for the best in everybody!" commented Peggy, Second of the Swallow Patrol. "But whatever Jane likes to think, the gal on the hoss is an exhibitionist."

"And that's the final word!" murmured Karen, the fifth Guide reclining at ease on the sunbaked grass. "Peggy hath spoken—but for once I agree with her!"

The girl on the pony was not too far away to be seen clearly by the Guides. She gave no sign that she was aware of their presence in the field. Yet it was obvious to all the Guides except the charitable Jane that she was showing off her horsemanship for their express benefit.

After trotting and jumping the pony almost as if she were in the show-ring, she presently put it into a canter and circled the field. As she drew nearer to them the group of five Guides saw that she was about their own age, although in her jodhpurs and riding cap she looked older. She cast a disdainful glance at the

Guides, but it suddenly became fixed as if something about them had focussed her attention.

Abruptly she reined her pony in. "Are you Guides?" she exclaimed. Her face darkened. "Don't you know this field is private? You're trespassing! Get out!"

"We are. We do. We won't!" responded Peggy, promptly. "Do you mind very much, your highness?"

"Shut up, Peggy," ordered Jane. "It's quite all right," she said to the girl on the pony. "Colonel Dawes has given us permission to camp and wander about the estate. We're camping over there by the wood—just as a Patrol camp—our first, as a matter of fact."

"We're the Swallow Patrol," volunteered Karen chattily. "Who are you?"

"Colonel Dawes is my father. He wouldn't have given you permission to camp if I'd known anything about it, I can tell you. I don't like Guides! I—I hate them! I shall tell him that camp-fires are dangerous, with everything as dry as tinder. He'll order you off! Gee-up, Bonny!"

Without another glance at the Guides, she flicked the pony with her riding crop and set the animal into a spirited gallop.

"What a charmer!" murmured Peggy. "Did you notice the old-fashioned courtesy, girls?"

"She hates Guides, she said," observed Karen.

"I wonder why——?" began Jane, and then broke off. "Listen!"

"It sounds like a loud-speaker."

It *was* a loud-speaker. Although too far away for the Guides to see it clearly, they caught the flash of sunlight on the metallic roof of a distant car that was

58

cruising along the lane that ran alongside the far end of the field. They couldn't make out what the amplified voice was saying, but the strident tones struck a discordant note in the rural quietude.

"Funny to have a loud-speaker car along country lanes like these," remarked Brenda. "What on earth d'you think—Goodness, look at that pony!"

Whatever the voice through the loud-speaker was saying, there was no doubt of its effect on the pony Colonel Dawes' daughter was riding. The girl had ridden the pony to the far side of the field, on the other side of the bordering hedge of which ran the lane along which the loud-speaker car was moving. The amplified voice hit the spirited temperamental pony suddenly and forcefully, and it snorted, reared up—and then bolted.

The startled Guides jumped up as the pony raced in their direction, hooves thudding.

"Look out!" exclaimed Anne. "The pony's running away!"

"Like fury it is!" muttered Brenda.

"Yes, it is, and it looks terribly dangerous!" breathed Jane, gazing anxiously at the tearaway pony, which was rapidly closing the distance between itself and the Guides.

It became clear beyond a doubt that the animal, frightened by the sudden noise from the loud-speaker, was quite out of control. It was tearing across the field at a terrifying speed, hooves beating an ominous tattoo on the hard ground.

All five Guides were alarmed. The pony's rider seemed to be making desperate efforts to rein in her mount, but the animal thundered on.

"It's coming straight for us!" breathed Karen. "We'd better move!"

"Stop!" It was Jane who spoke, checking the threatened panic. She had foreseen the real danger. "The quarry!" she rapped out quickly. "The pony is swerving! It will go straight into the quarry! Come on—all of you—quick!"

Even as she spoke, she began to run towards the edge of the nearby quarry, at which the field ended abruptly. The quarry was not more than twenty or thirty feet deep, but it was unfenced, and a violent plunge into it by a runaway horse would bring disaster to horse and rider.

Jane didn't wait for the others, but the Patrol had been trained to obey orders promptly. They didn't at once grasp their P.L.'s purpose, but they were on her heels when Jane reached the lip of the quarry.

The pony was not far away, either. As Jane turned, she saw that the runaway was heading wildly for a point that would take it headlong into the quarry.

"Line up by me—quick!" she called to the Guides. "We must make a barrier along the edge. Spread out, clasp hands, and head the pony off!"

None of the Swallows answered or spoke. Brenda's face turned white, and Karen and Anne hesitated. Peggy, the Second, tight-lipped and tense, said quietly: "Come on!" and they followed her as she ran a few paces beyond Jane, clasped the P.L.'s extended hand, and stretched out her own for Brenda to grasp.

So, as the pony tore down on them, it was faced with a human fence ten arms'-length long.

All five Guides shut their eyes in desperate fear as the pony tore unchecked at them. Anna choked back a scream, and Karen breathed a prayer. Next instant it was all over. The pony came to a sharp stop, threw itself on its haunches, and violently unseated its rider, who pitched backwards over its tail to the ground and lay sprawled there in an undignified heap nearly at the feet of the Guides. The pony neighed loudly, then began to crop grass as if nothing had happened.

"Are you all right?" cried Jane anxiously, unclasping her hand from Peggy's and running to the fallen rider.

A furious red face lifted itself out of the jumbled heap on the ground, and a pair of angry eyes sparked fire at the Guides.

"You idiots! What on earth d'you mean by scaring my pony like that?"

"Scaring it?" yelled Peggy in amazement.

The other Guides were taken aback by the startling, utterly unexpected reaction of the rider. They stared at the girl in something like stupefaction.

"But—but we saved you—you'd have gone over into the quarry if we hadn't stopped you!" Jane burst out at length.

"Your pony was running away with you," added Karen.

"Don't talk nonsense!" The rider scrambled to her feet and began dusting herself down angrily. "I'd got Bonny under perfect control. I'd have turned her all right if you hadn't frightened the life out of her and made her buck me off. Just like Girl Guides! You're a lot of interfering busybodies, and I'll tell Daddy so." Without a further glance at the dumbfounded Guides, she limped off after the pony, which allowed itself to be caught and mounted again.

"Well, what d'you know about that?" breathed Anne, gazing blankly after the rider.

"I don't," said Brenda. "I'm beat."

"Of all the ungrateful minxes that girl takes the biscuit—tin and all," declared Karen, breathing hard.

"We risk being battered to pulp by a stampeding horse to save her from a leap of death into a quarry, and we're called interfering busybodies!" exclaimed Peggy.

"All I know is that it was easily the worst moment of my life," asserted Jane, with deep feeling. Suddenly she burst out laughing. "Well, we have to admit Miss Dawes has got nerve! She knows perfectly well the pony was running away and that she hadn't a chance of stopping it, but she dislikes Guides so much that she turns it into an opportunity for blaming us!"

"Well, it's the last time I risk my precious young life and limbs to stop a runaway horse," stated Brenda emphatically. "This is definitely my first and last good turn in the horsy world!"

"Mine too!" agreed Anne.

"Come on," chuckled Jane. "We'd better beetle back to camp and console ourselves with a cup of tea."

Jane and Peggy were experienced campers, but for the others the weekend Patrol camp on Colonel Dawes' estate was their first taste of camp life. With the weather hot and sunny and the camp beautifully sited on the edge of a meadow close to a coppice all the Patrol were enjoying themselves hugely. Colonel Dawes' daughter's hostility amused rather than disturbed the Guides, but Jane cautioned the Patrol against inflaming it if they should meet her again. Colonel Dawes had given permission for a weekend Patrol camp through the District Commissioner, who was a personal friend of his, and Jane had heard that there was a likelihood of the whole Company being allowed to camp on the estate later on in the summer.

The Colonel paid the camp a visit just before dusk. All the Guides liked him at once. He was pleasant, unassuming and friendly, although, as they presently learned, carrying rather a heavy burden of worry about with him.

"My housekeeper told me you were settled in and were looking after yourselves successfully, so I won't pretend I've come to see that you're all right," he said. "The fact is, my daughter Barbara is convinced you're going to set my woods ablaze with sparks from your camp-fire and has also accused you of scaring her pony into giving her a toss. So I thought I'd better have a look at such dangerous guests!" He smiled at them as he spoke, but the Guides sensed a sadness behind his light tones.

"We'll be most careful not to do any damage of any kind, by fire or anything else," Jane assured him. "Guide camping rules are very strict, and Guides are taught to leave nothing behind but their thanks."

"And Barbara's pony—what about that?" asked the Colonel.

"It was running away with her," Jane told him quietly. "We all agree about that. I'm sure we couldn't be mistaken about it, sir. We linked hands to turn it from going into the quarry."

"Then I offer you my sincere thanks, even if Barbara doesn't," said the Colonel. "Barbara's a pretty good horsewoman, and I imagine it hurt her pride to be thrown."

"The pony was scared by a loud-speaker in a car," volunteered Peggy. "We heard it from the far side of the field."

"Ah! That must have been the police patrol car that's been going round the countryside warning people that a garage in the town had sold some petrol as paraffin. I hope to goodness they've found whoever bought it—it could be rather dangerous. You haven't an oil-stove of any sort for which you need paraffin, have you?"

Jane assured him that all their cooking was done over a camp-fire and that they were in no danger from petrol supplied as paraffin.

"That's a relief, anyway!" The Colonel rose. "By the way—" he hesitated a little—"I'd be very happy if you should happen to make friends with **my** daughter. She's rather in need just now of—er—good company."

"We'd be very glad for her to join us at any time," said Jane quickly. "We'll make her **very** welcome, won't we, girls?"

"Of course!"

"Please invite her to our camp, Colonel Dawes," said Peggy.

"Thank you," said the Colonel gratefully. "I will. 'Fraid she's got a bit of a grudge against Guides, but I think she'd soon pull in with you, and I'll tell her you said she'd be welcome. Goodnight!"

"If you ask me," said Peggy, gazing thoughtfully after his tall, upright figure, "Colonel Dawes has got quite a handful of daughter in Barbara."

Jane nodded. "But it's up to us to lend him a hand with her if we can, eh? He's jolly nice."

All the Patrol agreed with her on that point. If they had known of the dark act of vengeance Barbara Dawes was plotting against them, however, they would have thought much less of their chances of making friends with her.

Barbara's hatred of the Guides dated back to her recent expulsion from her school Company. From her first entry into the Company she had been a problem. Disappointed at finding she could not at once be a Patrol Leader, she flouted authority and resisted discipline. Her Guider and her own Patrol Leader bore patiently with her for a long time, trying to kindle in her some spark of the spirit of Guiding, but the final break came when Barbara perpetrated an act that brought her very near to expulsion from the school. She stole away from the Company meeting one evening and pulled the school fire-alarm bell, starting a panic that resulted in injuries to several girls. She was suspended from the school for the remainder of the term and dismissed from the Guide Company. So it was that she was riding her pony on her father's estate weeks before schools had broken up.

Barbara was vengeful. What she fancied was her humiliation at being run away with by her mettlesome pony and then thrown in front of the Guides fanned her hostility into flame. She longed to get her own back on the Guides by having them turned off the estate in disgrace and forbidden to camp there again. Then she saw the way. It was simple, even crude;

C

there was nothing guileful or subtle about Barbara. If the Guides' camp-fire should chance to set the tinder-dry undergrowth of the adjoining coppice alight, as sparks from it could, Colonel Dawes would be finally convinced that Guides camping on his estate were a danger.

The Guides' fire, as a matter of fact, was sited well clear of any inflammable vegetation, was modest in size, and safely ringed round with stones. Even Barbara, surveying it from the cover of the coppice, had to admit that there was no likelihood at all of any sparks flying off and igniting dry leaves or ferns.

"Daddy won't know that, though, when a coppice has gone up in flames," she told herself maliciously.

As she rode her pony through the woods and meadows surrounding the camp, she kept a watchful eye on the movements of the Patrol, and one afternoon saw her chance. Riding her pony back by a round-about route, she left it on the farthest side of the coppice, then crept stealthily through the undergrowth. There was only one Guide in sight. It was Karen, who was preparing tea. Barbara had seen Jane and another Guide, Brenda, going towards the village, evidently for supplies. Peggy and Anne were wooding a short distance from the camp. Karen put a billycan on the fire, then went back into the tent. Kneeling, Barbara scooped some brittle twigs and dry leaves together in a heap, then drew matches from a pocket of her jodhpurs, struck one, and applied the flame to the little pile. Flame flared up instantly, and flickered at once to the parched brown grass around.

Barbara did not wait. It was obvious that the flame

would spread without the aid of a further match—and with fearful swiftness.

Stooping to keep well out of sight if the Guide in the tent should look in her direction, Barbara ran silently back through the coppice and stopped only when she reached her pony. Mounting it, she turned it along one of the green paths that wound invitingly under the overhanging limbs of the beautiful oak and beech wood known as the Old Wood. This ended alongside the lane to the village, and it was Barbara's intention to ride through the wood and then turn into the lane and canter on to the village. This was a safety measure to give her an alibi, should one by any mischance be needed.

But she didn't reach the lane.

Halfway through the wood, she heard a curious, ominous crackling noise. She halted the pony to listen more closely.

"Funny! Well, it must be the fire! It's spread pretty fast. It's——"

She stopped. She stared. For an instant she couldn't believe her eyes. Then her face paled, drained a ghostly white. Horrified, hypnotised, she gazed ahead, almost refusing to credit what she saw.

Ahead stretched a wide, thin red wall of fire, which was moving slowly towards her across the whole width of the wood.

Relentlessly the truth forced itself into her consciousness. The Old Wood ahead of her was on fire, blazing along its entire breadth. She had set fire to the coppice behind her—a long way behind her, close to the Guides' camp. By some devilish affinity the wood in front of her, in the opposite direction to the one she had fired, had caught alight!

Barbara couldn't move. She sat the pony, paralysed.

But the pony moved. Suddenly startled and affrighted by the whiff of fire, it let out a loud, shrill, fear-stricken neigh. Then it leapt madly away along the path that ran at right-angles to the one along which Barbara had steered it. Barbara had no chance of controlling or guiding it. Terrified by the sight and fumes of the advancing fire, the animal tore blindly and irresistibly through the wood away from the horror, towards the safety of the open meadow.

But disaster struck its rider within seconds. So furious was the pony's pace that Barbara had no time to duck her head as the low-hanging limbs of the bordering trees rushed at her. Her reinforced riding cap saved her from a cracked skull, but she catapulted backwards like a ninepin as the gnarled bough of an overhanging oak cracked her hat open with a stunning blow and stretched her senseless.

The pony rushed on, leaving Barbara on the grassy track in the path of the fire.

Jane and Brenda were returning from the village with butter and eggs.

"My goodness!" exclaimed Jane. "It looks as if the whole wood's ablaze!"

They broke at once into a run. The same thought was in both their minds—to raise the alarm at the house and make sure that the Patrol tent was moved out of danger. It was clear that the fire had a destructive grip on the Old Wood. Smoke billowed out in

68

dense clouds, and the flames roared ferociously. Jane, not knowing that Barbara had deliberately set the small coppice adjoining the Patrol afire, did not visualise any immediate danger to their tent, as the flames had not yet swept beyond the Old Wood, although it was only a matter of time before they did so and then, unless somehow checked, leapt the gap between the wood and the campside coppice. But she intended to transfer camp to a safe site and make sure that Colonel Dawes or his housekeeper at the Hall, which was within a stone's throw of the camp, knew of the blaze and had called the fire-brigade.

Careless of likely damage to the eggs they were bringing back, the Guides raced at top speed across the meadow bordering the Old Wood. About halfway across, both were startled by the sudden appearance of a galloping horse. It burst out of the smoky wood like some phantom steed in an old legend, its hooves making no sound on the thick mossy carpet of the wood. Its ears were laid back in terror and its eyes were dilated. It did not pause, but tore straight on past the Guides, riderless and fear-stricken.

Jane gripped Brenda's arm.

"My goodness, Brenda, that looks like Barbara Dawes' pony! I'm sure it is!"

"Well, what if it is? I don't see—— Oh, golly, Jane, you don't mean—you don't think——?"

"It's possible—it's even likely! The pony's got a saddle on. If Barbara was riding it and it took fright and threw her, as it did when that loud-speaker suddenly blared out——" Jane stopped and her voice was very grave as she added quietly: "Barbara would be in the wood, perhaps unable to get out."

"Oh, Jane, what are we going to do?" Brenda's cheeks had paled.

"You run on and warn the Patrol and tell Peggy to get word of the fire to the house without a moment's delay—just in case they don't know about it. Then come back here, all of you. I may need your help. Anyway, I'm going in to see if Barbara's anywhere about."

"Oh, Jane, you mustn't—it's dangerous! Barbara may have come out, and you might——"

"A Guide is obedient," interrupted Jane, smiling. "So scram, dear Brenda!"

"Oh, Jane——" Brenda was almost in tears—"you won't go where the fire is, will you—you will be careful, won't you?"

"The quicker you go, the quicker you'll be back to pull me out if I'm getting toasted, so—run!"

Brenda ran. She perceived the sense of Jane's reasoning.

Jane ran too—but into the wood at the point where Barbara's pony had rushed out. She fell back, choking, as a plume of acrid smoke struck her, but it swept past her within a few seconds and she ran on. But the sight that met her eyes as the path took her from the fringe into the depths of the wood made her heart miss a beat. Red tongues of fire, like living things, were licking swiftly towards her from the right, devouring the dry vegetation that carpeted the wood and leaping up the trees like serpents' coils. Before her appalled gaze a beech-tree, its trunk almost burnt through, suddenly came crashing down, sending up a shower of sparks.

Jane stopped, shaken. Then, cupping her hands over

her mouth, she called out: "Barbara Dawes, are you there? Are you in the wood? Barbara! Barbara Dawes!"

There was no answer. Jane didn't wait to call again. She hurried on, following the path, which was still clearly defined. She was feeling the intense heat of the fire now, and the smoke almost suffocated her when it swept over and enveloped her.

She kept on, but she knew from the speed with which the fire was advancing that she would soon have to turn and race back along the path if she was to avoid being caught up in it, or, alternatively, run before the fire at right-angles to the path.

Then, running round a bend in the path, she saw Barbara.

The girl was lying on her back across the path. Her riding hat was several yards away from her head—smashed, Jane noticed quickly. Her face was deathly white and her eyes were closed.

"Barbara!" shouted Jane. "Barbara Dawes!"

She bent over her. Barbara was still breathing, but she was unconscious.

Jane looked swiftly round at the ominous red zig-zag crackling and hissing at a frighteningly short distance from where she stood. She thought of racing back to the meadow and bringing the Patrol in to help convey Barbara to safety, but she realised that the on-coming tide of fire would reach and engulf the helpless girl before she could get back to her again. There was only one thing to do, and Jane set to work to do it. Somehow, alone, she must haul Barbara to safety.

Stooping, she placed her arms round the girl's

shoulders and under her armpits, lifted her, and then, step by step, dragged her back along the path.

It was a nightmare journey, painful and laborious. Her pace was slow. Barbara was heavy and a dead weight. As the fire drew nearer, the heat and the smoke became more intense. After fifty yards Jane was sobbing with the sheer strain of it. Her face was black with smoke, and drawn, and her eyes were stinging and streaming. Her back felt as if it was going to break. She stopped, because she simply could not keep going, but she kept her arms about Barbara, fearing that she might not find strength to lift her again if she let her down. After a moment she moved backwards again, supporting the dragging, inert weight of the unconscious girl. But the fire was getting dangerously near now, and Jane, with a quick glance at the lurid red tongues of flame that darted into clumps of fern and tussocks of grass and now and again plumed up in vivid consuming torches of fire, knew that unless she increased her pace the fire would engulf her and Barbara. And she couldn't increase her rate of progress! She was giving all of her strength and stamina to the task of pulling Barbara to safety, and the ultimate of her effort had been reached.

She paused again, then again went on. Smoke suddenly billowed over her and she had to let Barbara down and put her hands over her mouth and eyes to save herself from suffocation. At the same time she dropped to the ground, realising that the smoke was drifting above Barbara and leaving her largely untouched.

When the cloud thinned out, she struggled up, took hold of Barbara again, and resumed the slow backward journey. But she was losing the race. The crackling, hissing zigzags of fire were seething through the vegetation behind her and across the path. She glanced anxiously round. A young tree close to the path was ablaze. So was the undergrowth around it. It was roaring like a furnace. The way to the meadow would soon be cut off—she and Barbara would be trapped.

Desperately, Jane increased her rate of progress a fraction, but the fire was sending continuous clouds of smoke before it, and these rolled inexorably towards Jane and blanketed her. Suddenly she stumbled and almost fell. She hung on grimly to Barbara's inert body and somehow kept her feet, but she was almost spent. Her breath was coming in choking gasps, and the awful recognition was dawning upon her that she was not going to win through, that the fire and the smoke and the heat were too much for her, that she had lost the race to safety. Her last remaining shreds of strength began to slip away from her. Her knees sagged under her; she felt herself collapsing . . . then through the smoke and haze and the swimming heat came voices . . .

"There she is!"

"It's Jane! She's got Barbara! Hold on, Jane— we're coming!"

Jane couldn't hold on. She knew, with a great upsurge of thankfulness, that she didn't have to any longer. Dazed, bemused and exhausted as she was, she recognised those voices. The Swallow Patrol had arrived.

Colonel Dawes looked round the circle of Guides,

who were in various stages of striking camp, and smiled. "I'm sorry to see you going," he said, "but I hope to renew acquaintance with you in the summer. I am going to offer the District Commissioner a site of her own choice on the estate. What did you say the name of your Patrol was?"

"The Swallows," Jane told him.

"The Swallows' first camp—a very memorable one it's been!" The Colonel's grave, kindly eyes rested on each of the five Guides in turn. "Barbara's narrow escape has changed her outlook—and I mean your courageous rescue of her, Jane. She has been a deep anxiety to me for years. I've not been able to do anything with her; neither has anyone else. But this experience has done something to her. She told me it had, and I'm very happy to realise it's true. She asked if you'd go and see her before you leave, Jane."

"I will, with pleasure," replied Jane.

"She told me she's got something personal to say to you." The Colonel smiled. "She admitted to me that the pony was out of control when you stopped it from going into the quarry. I'd like to thank you all for that too, very deeply."

"I'll go along to Barbara now."

Barbara was still in bed. Both she and Jane had suffered some hurt from burns, though nothing serious. Barbara, however, had sustained a heavy fall, which, combined with a condition of acute emotional upset, had taken toll of her.

She looked up eagerly at Jane.

"Did Daddy tell you to come? There's something I want to tell you, Jane, something I've got to confess. You know how that fire started, don't you?"

74

"Yes, your father told us. The motorist who'd parked on the roadside just by the Old Wood was the customer who'd been given petrol in mistake for paraffin, and when he used it in his Primus stove to boil up water for tea it burst into flames and set the grass and then the wood ablaze."

"I know that." Barbara nodded. "It's true, but it might have been me."

"What d'you mean—it might have been? It wasn't, and that's that."

"But I did start a fire—close to your tent. I wanted to burn it down." Quietly, ashamedly, Barbara told what she had done. "Now I've got to tell Daddy," she finished, "and—and I can't bear to do it, because it'll hurt him so to think I'd done such a dreadful thing and risked burning his woods down and—and——" She stopped, and covered her face.

"I should forget the whole thing," Jane said practically. "There's no reason why he should know. It belongs to the past, and that's where I should leave it. It wouldn't have burnt the woods down, anyway, or even the tent, because Peggy, who's Second in the Swallows, is quick on the uptake. She spotted the blaze before it got a hold around the camp and organised the other two and beat it out with branches."

"Did she? Oh, that was fine!" exclaimed Barbara thankfully. "And do you really think I needn't tell Daddy?"

Jane nodded. "There's somebody else I'd like to tell, though, if you'll let me—Peggy. She's under a cloud— a big black cloud. She thinks the fire was started by *her* fire! She feels terrible about it. It's a reflection on her skill as a camper. So do please let me clear her good name!"

"I can't refuse that, can I?" Barbara smiled and held out her hand. "I'll never forget what you've done for me. When I get back to school I'm going to ask to rejoin the Guides."

Jane clasped Barbara's left hand in a firm Guide shake.

EAGLES ON THE LINE

ONE of the things that had bothered Jill and Liza since joining the Guides was how to be of service to others. Both were new members of the 1st Courtenay Company and were keen on carrying out the Guide Law to the full. Both were members of the Eagle Patrol.

"There's not much in the way of service you can do in a village, is there?" said Jill.

"I found that in Brownies," said Liza. "We both did. We were supposed to do a good turn every day, but it was a job to find anybody who wanted a good turn done."

One afternoon Jill was on her way to Liza's house for tea, after which both girls would go on to Guide meeting. So, although it was long before the time for the meeting, Jill was in uniform. The afternoon was wintry, and there was a dusting of snow on the lane from the village, and icicles in the hedgerows.

A gang of boys were coming noisily towards Jill up the lane, talking and joking and dragging home-made sledges behind them. They were making for Pollard Hill. A sharp knocking on the window of the only cottage in the lane attracted Jill's attention and made the boys turn their heads. An old lady beckoned urgently to them and then came hobbling out of the front door and down to the gate.

"I wonder if one of you boys would do something for me," she said. "I haven't a spot of coal in the house, and I can't get any delivered. The coal merchants tell me there's plenty of coal in the station yard, but they say they can't get any out to me for two or three weeks; they're so snowed under with orders and are short of delivery men. If one or two of you bigger boys would fetch me a little on your sledge I'd be so grateful. I'm too old to fetch it myself."

"Sorry, ma'am, but we're going sledging on Pollard Hill," said Fred Starky, one of the bigger boys—and he moved off as quickly as he could.

"I've got nobody to ask, you see, or I wouldn't trouble you," pleaded the old lady to the other boys. "I would give you something for yourself, of course," she added, "gladly."

But most of the boys were already moving hurriedly on after Fred Starky.

"Come on, Snowy," Bill Higgins called back to Johnny Snow, one of the younger boys, who was standing looking at the old lady. "If you want to ride on my sledge you'll have to help pull it up the hill."

"O.K.," said Snowy, who Jill thought for a moment was going to answer the old lady's plea for help. "I'm coming, Bill." He hurried after Bill Higgins.

Jill made up her mind. Hurrying over to the old lady at the gate, she said, "I'll fetch you some coal. Liza will help me. She's got an old push-chair that her daddy uses for moving garden rubbish, and we could bring the coal in that."

"You're a very kind girl to want to help me." The old lady looked rather doubtfully at Jill, who wasn't very big. "Are you sure you could manage it? It would really be doing me a service. I don't know what I'm going to do for a fire if I don't get some coal soon."

"Liza and I will do it," Jill assured her. "We'll have plenty of time to get the coal before Guide meeting."

"Then I will give you the money for half a hundredweight," said the old lady, opening her purse. "I don't think you'll be able to manage more. Don't strain yourselves. Just bring what you can. I'll be grateful for only a few lumps."

Taking the money from the old lady, who said her name was Mrs. Pearson, Jill ran off down the lane and hardly stopped till she reached Liza's house.

Liza, who had changed into her Guide uniform, was eager to do a service for the old lady, and her mother agreed that she could go. Her mother said they ought to be able to manage half a hundredweight all right in the old push-chair, although it was rather a long way from the station to push it.

"I know!" said Liza, as they set off for the station yard. "Let's take it in turns to give each other a push."

Riding in the old push-chair or running behind it was great fun, although both girls slipped and fell several times on the slippery surface of the lane. They were glowing with warmth by the time they reached the station yard.

The yardman at the station weighed out half a hundredweight of coal and shovelled it into a sack he found for them. The sack dropped down and wedged itself firmly between the two arms of the push-chair. The Guides were satisfied that it wouldn't fall out even if the push-chair went over a big bump.

"There you are," said the yardman. "I only 'ope you'll be able to drag it out when you get to the other end."

"We'll manage somehow," said Jill. "We'll find

someone to help at the other end if we can't hoist the sack out by ourselves."

"It isn't all that heavy," said Liza cheerfully.

"Off we go, then!" chortled Jill.

"Let's take a handle each," said Liza.

The loaded push-chair was a lot heavier than they had expected it to be, but they managed to push it up the rise from the station and into the snowy lane that led alongside the railway. They had gone some distance along this when they saw two youths coming towards them.

"Oh, dear!" murmured Liza. "Here's that Digger Brown!"

"And Charley Collins!" said Jill.

Digger and Charley were well known to both girls and to most of the other girls in the district. They were by way of being toughs, and were fond of breaking up the games of other boys and generally being aggressive.

"Hey, Charley, look there!" cried Digger, when he saw the sack of coal in the push-chair. "They're carrying coal in a push-chair. I think they ought to give us a ride, don't you?"

"I need one; I'm tired out," grinned Charley.

"We're taking coal to an old lady," Jill told them, "and she's waiting for it."

"Girl Guides do a good turn every day, don't they?" said Charley. "We need a ride, so tip the coal out, Digger, an' then they can push us home."

Digger grabbed at the coal with both hands. The load, however, was too firmly wedged to be moved easily, and so Digger sat on it and called on his companion to give him a ride.

"You're not to!" shouted Jill.

"You'll break the push-chair!" cried Liza, and tried to pull Charley's arm away from the handles, which he had seized.

Charley gave her a shove that sent her sprawling. Then, with a whoop he charged down the lane with the push-chair, with Digger seated on top of the sack of coal, waving and shouting.

Jill helped Liza up, and the two ran after the youths. Charley, however, was racing the push-chair along at a pace that left the Guides behind until, all of a sudden, he slipped on a glassy patch of road. As he lost his balance, the push-chair flew forward out of his hands, and Digger pitched out and hit the hard surface of the lane with a force that shook the breath out of him. The push-chair, diverted from its course, shot across the frozen grass-verge and straight through a gap in the fence above the railway embankment.

"Stop it!" shouted Jill gazing, horrified, at the push-chair, which was leaping down the steep embankment towards the railway track.

She and Liza raced towards the fence, but were only in time to see the push-chair turn a somersault on the cinders at the foot of the embankment and land upside-down across the railway-track, with the sack of coal still firmly wedged in it.

"Oh, blimey, that's torn it!" muttered Charley, gazing down at the push-chair.

Digger scrambled to his feet. "Come on, Charley," he called. "We'd better scram."

"You can't leave the push-chair across the rails!" cried Jill.

"Please pull it back up to the lane," pleaded Liza.

But Digger and Charley turned and ran.

"What had we better do, Liza?" asked Jill, in dismay—"go back to the station and tell somebody about it?"

"Yes, I should think so," replied Liza. "We might be able to move it ourselves, but——" She stopped, her cheeks turning a shade paler. A loud click had sounded a little way down the railway track. Out of the corner of her eye she saw a signal-arm swing upward. "Did you see that signal move, Jill?" she asked in a dismayed whisper. "Does it mean there's a train due?"

Jill nodded, her own cheeks pale now. "I believe so. Liza, we—we can't leave the push-chair across the lines. It might wreck the train."

Liza looked at her, wide-eyed. "D'you mean we—we ought to go down and—and pull it off?"

Jill nodded dumbly. Stooping through the broken fence, she began to slither down the embankment. "We must get it off the line before the train comes, Liza."

Liza hesitated. Then, cautiously, she followed Jill, slipping and sliding down the frozen slope.

At the foot they grasped a handle each and heaved at the push-chair, but they couldn't move it.

"It's terribly heavy," panted Jill.

"It's because the coal's underneath, I expect," said Liza.

They tried again—and again—but the sack of coal was a dead weight underneath the seat and was in some way caught under the rail. They couldn't shift it.

"I know," said Jill. "We'll have to pull the coal out of the sack from underneath."

"Be quick, then," said Liza. "The train will be along soon."

Dropping to their knees, the Guides thrust their hands underneath the push-chair and pulled out the topmost lumps of coal.

"We mustn't waste them," said Liza, and threw her lump on to the cinder-path between the track and the embankment.

Jill followed suit. In quite a short time they had emptied the sack. The coal was scattered over the cindered path. They were both filthy with coal-dust by the time they had finished.

"We ought to be able to move the push-chair now," said Jill.

"Why there's the train!" cried Liza, in sudden fright. "I can hear it coming!"

Jill turned pale. "We must pull the push-chair off!"

She heaved at the frame of the push-chair, while Lesley grasped the handles. It didn't budge. The girls stared at each other.

"Pull harder!" cried Jill desperately.

"I'm scared!" gasped Liza, but she pulled just the same—as hard as she could. As she did so, the train came into view in the distance.

"Pull again, then!" panted Liza. "It's moving."

They heaved together, and quite suddenly the push-chair came right side up. Swiftly, thankfully, the Guides lifted it over the rails and on to the cindered path.

"Get right over by the embankment, Liza," urged Jill.

The train was looming large now. They had cleared the line only just in time.

The roar of the train grew rapidly louder as they carried the push-chair over to the embankment. They flattened themselves back, and the train thundered past, coach after coach.

Jill turned a grimy face to Liza, whose white teeth smiled triumphantly back at her out of a face smudged with coal-dust.

"We'd better pick up all the coal and put it back in the sack," she said.

They didn't have to drag the coal and the push-chair back up the embankment, however, for the guard of the train had seen them from his van and reported the fact to the station manager, who sent a porter to investigate.

Jill and Liza had to go back with the porter to the station, where they told the station manager all that had happened.

"You'd no business to be on the railway, of course," the station manager said sternly. Looking at the two tired and very dirty Guides, his face relaxed. "But you acted very bravely and you may have saved the train from being derailed. Now, the thing is to get you home."

"But the coal——?" began Jill.

"Don't worry about that," the station manager said. "My porters will load it up for you and carry your push-chair up the embankment. I'm sure you'll want to deliver the coal to Mrs. Pearson, as you promised you would, but I'll have a word with the coal-merchant and see if I can arrange for a proper load to be sent to her tomorrow. I think I can."

That was very satisfactory to Jill and Liza, who told the good news to Mrs. Pearson when they delivered the half-hundredweight of coal. The old lady stood horri-fied at the sight of two quite filthy Guides on her doorstep, but invited them in and helped them clean themselves up when she heard of their adventure.

An exciting end to their act of service came in the form of a letter from British Rail, which thanked them for what they did and praised them for their bravery.

"I think," said their Guider, when they showed her the letter, "we ought to make a frame for this and hang it up to remind the Company that there are all kinds of ways for a Guide to give service—even if not always quite as thrilling as yours, Jill and Liza."

DANGER TRAIL

"I DON'T really want to go bird-watching with you, Corinne." Lesley shook her head as she turned the pages of the local weekly newspaper. "Bird-watching is so tame."

"It isn't; it's thrilling," asserted her P.L. calmly. "I've located a woodpecker's nest, and I'm hoping to see the babies soon. You'll enjoy an afternoon in the woods, Lesley."

"Oh, I'll come. Perhaps I could do some stalking if I get bored. Now, stalking attracts me—ah, this is more like it! Listen to this, Corry!" She stabbed the newspaper with her finger. " 'Safe-blowers' gelignite store found in Surrey sandpit—Police ask public to aid in search for explosives.' " Leslie looked up excitedly. "That would be something to search for! It says here that the police believe that quantities of the explosive used by safe-breakers are hidden in disused quarries and similar places in country areas. I say, Corry, do you realise we're in Surrey and that there are lots of out-of-the-way spots where explosives could be stored? Wouldn't it be super if we . . . ?"

"No, I don't think it would," Corinne interrupted. "I'd much rather bird-watch peacefully in the woods than stumble on a store of—what did you say it was called?—ah, yes, gelignite—or fall foul of a gang of bank-robbers."

"What are a few blown safes compared with a woodpecker's nest? What time do we start?"

"That's what you began looking in the paper for," Corinne pointed out. "There's a note of new bus times for summer services there somewhere."

Having found the information about the changed bus times, the two Guides fixed up to meet after lunch and travel to Playden Woods, a very large tract of woodland and heath that provided rich facilities for the Guides of the 3rd Dorford Company for tracking, stalking, nature-study and Guiding activities generally.

Corinne owned a pair of binoculars, and she was blissfully happy some hours later as she crouched in the sun-speckled undergrowth of Playden Woods with the glasses trained on a dark hole high up in the trunk of an aged beech-tree. Lesley, beside her, carried on a murmured conversation until her P.L.'s hand closed suddenly over her arm and her voice whispered softly: "Sh! Look, there it is!"

Looking up, Lesley caught an exciting fleeting glimpse of a large green bird with a red head clinging to the bark of the beech. Hers was only a transitory view, because the thud of approaching feet suddenly disturbed the quietude and alarmed the woodpecker, which ran swiftly up the trunk in a spiral and disappeared into its hole.

"Oh, what bad luck!" murmured Corinne. "We'd have had a lovely view of him. Did you see him, Lesley?"

Lesley nodded. "Yes, but only just. I must say I could wish the owner of those clodhoppers somewhere!"

Screened by ferns and undergrowth, the Guides were hidden from the view of the owner of the "clodhoppers", but they could see him clearly. He was carrying an axe.

Lesley nudged Corinne. "Not content with frightening the woodpecker, he's going to chop the tree down!"

"Not this one, I think."

The man passed on out of view of the girls, who, however, looked at each other in surprise as the thud of an axe against wood began to break the silence of the woods.

"He's using it on one of them," said Lesley. "This is where I get some stalking practice in. Coming, Corry?"

Corinne sighed and nodded. She was curious to know why the axeman was felling a tree.

To the surprise of the Guides, however, they discovered it was not a tree to which the axe was being laid. It was a signpost! They came within sight just in time to see the post fall. What followed was even more perplexing. The axeman lifted the post bodily and carried it into deep undergrowth and tossed it out of sight.

"Well, what's he do that for?" demanded Lesley.

Corinne shook her head, puzzled.

The axeman's next actions were even more curious. He proceeded to obliterate the path along which the signpost had pointed by uprooting bushes and clumps of fern and scattering them over it. He took great care to dispose of the vegetation realistically. At length, satisfied that a casual eye would not suspect the existence of the path, he cast a final critical glance over his

88

handiwork, then picked up the axe and strode away.

The two Guides looked at each other in silent inquiry. Then, by mutual consent, they made for the patch of vegetation into which the signpost had disappeared.

Reaching it, Corinne turned the name-board over. Then she whistled softly. The lettering on the board had been blurred by weather, but was still readable. It said: TO THE QUARRY.

"It can't be—what I read in the paper, can it?" Lesley's voice was quite shaky as she asked the question. "You know—the explosives?"

"A gelignite store? Oh, no!" Corinne gazed in almost horrified protest at her companion.

"Why not? He was acting very suspiciously. Why should he want to chop down a signpost pointing to a quarry and go to all the trouble of covering up a footpath if it wasn't to stop people going to the quarry? And why should he so badly want to keep people away if he isn't hiding something?"

"Perhaps it's—well, it may be unsafe."

"Unsafe, my foot! Shall I tell you the real reason? Because that newspaper report might make people want to go to the quarry, if they saw a signpost pointing to it. That's why he took it down and blotted out the path! And that must mean the quarry contains something—sinister."

Firmly, Corinne took her arm. "Whether there's anything in what you say or whether there isn't, you're not going there, Lesley Maynard! If there is something in what you say, it would be very dangerous; if there isn't, you'd be much better occupied bird-watching. So there! Now come on! Our woodpecker may be back on duty!"

Reluctantly, Lesley, allowed herself to be persuaded back to the beech-tree, under which Corinne once again ensconced herself with the binoculars to her eyes.

But their privacy was not to be long enjoyed. The woodpecker had just made its reappearance, and Corinne was hissing a low warning to Lesley to freeze when the stillness of the woods was shattered by movements in the undergrowth and the sound of distant voices.

The woodpecker vanished as suddenly as it had appeared.

"Well, would you believe it?" exclaimed Lesley disgustedly. "For the second time, and just as he was about to start pecking operations!"

Corinne lowered her binoculars resignedly.

"They'll have to install traffic-lights in the woods if this goes on," grumbled Lesley. "Sounds as if there's a horde coming this time. If they're going to look for more signposts to cut down——" She broke off. "Oh, gosh!"

"What is it?" demanded Corinne.

"It isn't what is it, but who is it! It's Guides, that's who! They're our lot, Corry!"

"By our lot I presume you mean Guides of the 3rd Dorford Company. Yes, it's the Skylarks, all right—or three of them."

The Skylark Patrol burst into view through the trees, but they were too busy circling about searching the ground intently to notice Corinne and Lesley even when they stood up. Corinne hailed them. Then Susan, their Second, ran up.

"I say, Corinne, have you seen anything of Rachel? We've lost her completely. We're following a trail she's laid but it's petered out and we haven't a clue in which direction she's gone."

"Where did it peter out?" asked Corinne.

"Some way back. She made a twig arrow pointing this way along the path, but there's not another sign after that. I can't understand it."

"She hasn't passed while we've been here, and we came along from the opposite direction, but—by jove!"

"Thought of something?"

Corinne shook her head doubtfully. "It's only a possibility. The man who passed by covered up a footpath with bushes and ferns. Why, we don't know, but it just occured to me that he might have covered Rachel's tracking signs in the process."

"You mean that Rachel could have turned off along that path to the quarry—before we arrived here?" put in Lesley excitedly. "Gosh, you may be right there, Corry! The mystery man chopped down a signpost pointing the way to the quarry before camouflaging the path itself, Susan."

"The dickens he did! Why?"

"Goodness knows! But let's go and undo his handi-work and see if we can find Rachel's trail under-neath it."

Eagerly, the Skylarks followed Corinne and Lesley to the stump of the felled signpost and helped them fling aside the "camouflage" scattered over the foot-path by the axeman.

"My conscience is pricking me," declared Corinne. "We ought really to put it back after us, I suppose. The man may have covered up the path for a legitimate reason—though I can't think of one."

"Let's look for Rachel's tracking signs first, anyway," urged Lesley.

But no sign was exposed—which, however, meant little, since it could easily have got tossed away with the camouflage vegetation, or been obliterated in the process. Suddenly, however, Susan gave a shout. She had quested on along the path well beyond the point at which the "camouflage" ceased, and now she pointed triumphantly down at three sticks on the path.

"An arrow! You were right, Corry! It's Rachel's trail!"

"What are we waiting for?" asked Trixie, the youngest of the Skylarks, racing up. "Let's go!"

"Just a minute." Corinne frowned. "It might be—well, wise—to go cautiously."

"What are you hinting at?" demanded Susan.

"Corinne's absolutely right," declared Lesley emphatically. "There may be something fishy going on. I think there is. That man who covered up the path to the quarry doesn't want people to go there. Why? It looks as if he's hiding something."

"D'you mean there might be danger?" said Susan, then added sharply: "What about Rachel, then?"

There was an uneasy hush. The Guides looked doubtfully at each other.

"We'd better go," said Corinne briefly, "and very quietly."

Suiting the action to the words, she set off, swiftly

92

but silently, along the path, which was just discernible between the tall ferns. In silence the others followed, in single file. All five now were keyed-up. The hushed wood, still dappled in sunshine, had suddenly become sinister.

The path wound in serpentine fashion through the wood. To the Guides, anxious and worried about Rachel, it seemed endless. They met no one, and scarcely a sound above their own deadened footfalls disturbed the stillness. Through a wilderness of ferns sheltered by the delicate foliage of silver birches, they followed the twisting path. Their vision was bounded on all sides by trees, but at last the trees began to thin out and suddenly they came out on to open grassland, which, some distance ahead, dropped precipitously away into a deep quarry.

"I can see somebody there," remarked Bertha, the fifth Guide, shading her eyes with her hand. "Two figures, I think."

"Duck down!" said Susan sharply. "We're better not show ourselves—for a bit, anyhow."

"I can't really believe——" began Corinne, then stopped abruptly, as her binoculars focussed. "My goodness!"

"What is it?" asked Susan anxiously.

"There's a car at the top of the quarry, and two men are moving up towards it." She caught her breath sharply. "They're carrying something between them. It looks—it looks——"

"You don't mean—you can't mean—Rachel?" Susan whispered.

Corinne gave her the binoculars. "I can't be sure. It looks like a—a person."

"I believe it is Rachel!" exclaimed Susan. "I can't tell for sure, but I've got a nasty feeling it is. What's happened? Perhaps she—she fell into the quarry."

"Much more likely she's seen more than is good for her and was nabbed and nobbled," asserted Lesley. "That man with the axe didn't chop the signpost down and cover up the track because the quarry has suddenly become dangerous."

"There's no time to argue," put in Corinne decisively. "We've got to make sure first whether it is Rachel they're carrying. Keep away from the edge of the quarry and they won't see us. Now—make for the car—and hurry!"

With the P.L. leading the way, the Guides raced for the car. They had to take a semi-circular route along the top of the quarry and keep some distance from the edge to avoid being seen by the men. By the time the car came within their view again they saw that the men had reached it and deposited their burden inside it. Corinne stopped, sank down, and signalled to the others to follow suit.

"What do we do now?" breathed Lesley. "Rush 'em?"

"No sense in that—yet," murmured Corinne. "We don't know for certain it's Rachel. Wait! We'll take the car's number, just in case; then find out somehow —ah!"

The cause of her exclamation was the departure of one of the men. As if remembering something, he spoke to his companion and then set off at a run down the slope leading to a brick building at the base of the quarry. The second man, who had been about to climb into the driver's seat, turned and followed more slowly after the other, as if to meet him coming back and save him the trouble of returning the full distance.

"Now's our chance!" hissed Corinne. "As soon as he's out of sight I'm going to dash for the car. Will two of you—Bertha and Trixie—stay behind out of sight, in case you need to go for help? Susan and Lesley and I will rush for the car. For goodness' sake, don't let's get spotted! Now—run!"

Like hares, Corinne, Susan and Lesley raced for the car. If the driver, going down the slope, had turned his head he would have seen them, but they made no sound that drew his attention and in the space of seconds were peering through the side window of the car at the figure stretched out on the back seat.

"It is!" muttered Lesley.

"Rachel!" exclaimed Susan.

Rachel it was. White-faced, her eyes closed, she lay on her back on the seat. As Corinne opened the door and softly called her name, her eyes flickered open.

"Corinne!" she murmured faintly. "That man—he said I was spying—he threatened me—he——"

"Never mind that now," Corinne interrupted her. "Tell us when we get you out of here. Come on, Rachel—quick. Oh, gosh, I think she's fainted!"

She was right. Rachel had sunk back in a dead faint.

"Quick!" urged Susan. "The man will be back. Take her head, Corinne. Lesley and I will lift her out from here."

Sensibly, Trixie and Bertha, realising the need, ran up and helped to get Rachel out. As they started away with her, the first man came out of the building with something under his arm, which he passed to the car-driver.

"Hurry!" panted Susan. "We'll be spotted!"

"As soon as we reach cover drop down and keep absolutely still," gasped Corinne.

With Rachel a dead weight, the fern-brake twenty yards or so away seemed an almost unattainable goal, but at last they reached it. They had barely sunk down into its friendly shelter when the car-driver's head appeared above the lip of the quarry. The Guides held their breath as he ran to the car.

About to climb into the driving seat, he glanced at the back seat—and froze. The Guides heard his astounded exclamation: "Strike me blue! She's gorn!"

He looked around rather dazedly, then ran to the quarry path and down it, shouting: "Tom, Tom, the Girl Guide's gorn!"

"Now!" said Corinne urgently. "Let's get Rachel right into the woods! Quick!"

"What's up?" mumbled Rachel, opening her eyes.

"Never mind—we're getting you to safety! Hurry, girls!"

Quickly they bore Rachel towards the shelter of the nearest trees. They were just beginning to congratulate themselves on getting safely away when a loud, gruff, angry exclamation startled them to a halt. Out of the trees into which they were moving stepped the man with an axe!

"Girl Guides—another lot!" he snapped.

"This girl has been hurt; we can't stop," said Corinne quickly.

The man bent forward and looked at Rachel. "Why,

that's the girl I warned away from the quarry an hour or two ago! Hurt, you say? What happened to her——?'' He broke off and called loudly over the heads of the Guides. "Hi, Harry!"

Corinne groaned. The car-driver's head had just appeared at the top of the quarry path. One more minute and they would have been safely out of sight in the wood!

As Harry started to run towards them in answer to the axeman's call, Rachel murmured and struggled to get down. The Guides supported her.

Harry let out a shout of surprise as he came up and recognised Rachel as the girl who had so mysteriously vanished from the car.

"Why, that's her!" he cried, pointing to Rachel. "We left her in the car when Tom went to fetch her mac, and when we got back she'd gorn!''

"What's been going on, Harry?" demanded the man with the axe.

"She fell into the quarry, Mr. Groves." Harry nodded at Rachel. "Knocked herself out: might have been killed. Tom and me carried her into the old kiln, but she kept blacking out and so we reckoned we'd better run her to hospital. Then she disappeared, like I said."

"I'm all right now," murmured Rachel, feeling her head tenderly. "I wanted to lay a trail to beat the Patrol—along the path winding down into the quarry —but he stopped me.'' She indicated the man with the axe. "So I waited till he'd gone and then took another path."

"And came a cropper, eh?" snapped Mr. Groves. "I only hope you didn't——" He stopped, but Harry

D

put in: "She didn't fall anywhere near the birds, Mr. Groves. They ain't been disturbed."

"What birds?" said Corinne quickly.

"Never you mind——" began Mr. Groves, and then stopped. A brightly plumed bird was rising up from the quarry. The sunlight caught its yellow bib and green breast and outlined its long bill. Wonderingly, Corinne put her binoculars to her eyes and watched as it flew over the treetops; then she gave an excited cry.

"Why, it looks like—surely—surely it's a very rare bird! Is it—oh, it can't be!—is it a—a bee-eater?" She heard Mr. Groves groan. She swung round on him. "Is that why you cut down the signpost and covered the path to the quarry," she cried, "to keep people away from a rare bird?"

"There's a pair of 'em," admitted Mr. Groves. "Not for twenty-five years have bee-eaters nested in Britain. I'm a naturalist, and I determined not to let 'em be scared away by sightseers. That's why, when your trail-layer here told me other Girl Guides were tracking her, I ordered her off and did my best to keep the rest of you out. Harry and Tom have been helping me protect the bee-eaters by keeping guard until they've hatched out their family. Now you know—and I'm mighty sorry you do."

"Oh, but you needn't worry about us," Corinne assured him. "We wouldn't disturb them for anything —any of us—and we won't breathe a word about them, will we, Guides?"

"No!" chorused the Guides.

"But I'd love to keep an eye on them," added Corinne. "I'm working for the Bird Watcher badge and it would be wonderful to observe a rare bird like a bee-eater."

"So you're a bird-lover?" Mr. Groves held out his hand. "Shake! As a bird-lover you're welcome here at any time."

"Thank you," said Corinne, glowing with pleasure.

Lesley stepped across to her. "Take back what I said," she whispered in her ear. Seeing Corinne's inquiring look, she added with a grin: "Remember? Bird-watching is so tame!"

RECRUIT FOR THE RAVENS

"OH, bother, you're going off to those wretched Guides, Rosemary! I've got to take Baby Diane for a walk, and I hoped you'd come with me."

Rosemary smiled. "Don't worry, Mandy. Although I've got my Handbook I'm not going to Guides yet. I'm working for the Naturalist badge, and I was going along to the park to watch the birds and make notes about the park generally."

"Oh, good! I'll come along with you, then. It's a bore just pushing Diane, and—oh, dear—yes, young Roddy is coming as well."

Roddy was Mandy's young brother, whom she always found too mischievous to handle. Mandy wasn't very good with young children. Roddy came riding out of the gate on his tricycle.

"Mind you do as Mandy tells you, Roddy," his mother called after him.

Rosemary grinned. Roddy didn't usually do as Mandy told him. Mandy usually found taking Roddy and the baby for a walk something of an ordeal.

Rosemary wished she could persuade Mandy to join Guides, but Mandy was convinced that Guiding consisted mainly of learning to tie knots and going to camp once a year.

"You've no idea what a lot of interesting things we can do and learn about in Guides," Rosemary told her. "You'd enjoy Guides if you joined, Mandy. A lot depends on the kind of Guider a Company gets, but our Guider is super and thinks up all kinds of exciting activities for us."

Mandy didn't answer. Her attention was focussed on Roddy, who pedalled on ahead of the two girls as soon as he was out of his mother's sight.

"I can race you, Mandy!" he cried, and raced on along the pavement.

"Come back, Roddy!" cried Mandy, in alarm. "You're not to cross the road by yourself."

Roddy paid no heed. Racing on, he waved gleefully back at Mandy, and bumped straight on to a zebra crossing from the pavement. He knew he had to cross the road by way of the zebra crossing, but he didn't pause to look either way for traffic, and a car was approaching the crossing just as the boy dropped down on to it.

The car braked sharply, missing Roddy only by inches. Roddy reached the other side of the road safely, blissfully unaware of his narrow escape. The driver was furious, and shouted at Mandy, who had called after Roddy.

"Why don't you look after that child? I very nearly knocked him down."

"I'm—I'm very sorry!" muttered poor Mandy, who was badly shaken herself.

Still angry, the motorist started the engine again and drove off.

"I could bash that boy!" said Mandy wrathfully. "Mother would blame me if she knew, but Roddy never takes the slightest notice of anything I tell him to do."

Privately, Rosemary decided that Mandy wouldn't gain the Child Nurse badge if she were in Guides; she hadn't a notion of how to look after children.

Roddy was out of sight in the park by now. He pedalled happily down to the lake to feed the ducks. His mother had given him some bread when she knew Rosemary and Mandy were going to the park. By the lake he got off his trike and threw bread to the ducks and moorhens. This attracted swans, which Roddy didn't like.

"Shoo! Go away, you nasty swans," he shouted.

Looking round, he saw a thick stick, which he picked up and struck out with at the swans. Only the ducks and moorhens swam away. The female swan kept her distance, but the male stretched out a long neck and hissed angrily. Roddy continued to flail the stick, and suddenly the swan attacked, flapping its wings and rushing at Roddy.

Frightened now, the small boy turned and ran, pursued by the swan. Roddy could have outpaced the angry bird, but he tripped and fell.

Rosemary sized up the situation as she and Mandy came in sight of the lake. Dashing forward, she waved her hand and shouted at the swan, which turned, snaked out its long neck towards her and hissed menacingly. Her heart in her mouth, Rosemary thought the swan was going to lunge at her with its wicked-looking beak, but quite suddenly it spread its wings and flew off to the water.

Rosemary let out a gasp of relief. She picked Roddy up. The small boy, dirty and tearful, clung to her.

"I was frighted," he sobbed.

"So was I!" Rosemary admitted to herself. "It's

all right now, Roddy," she comforted the boy. "The swan's flown away. You're quite safe."

Mandy reached them. She began to scold Roddy, but Rosemary stopped her. "He's learned a lesson," she said. "I should leave it at that, Mandy."

"You were jolly brave, Rosemary," said Mandy. "Thanks for what you did."

Now that the danger was past, Mandy became aware of Roddy's appearance. The small boy was plastered with mud, and his face and hands were filthy.

"What on earth will Mum say?" muttered Mandy. "I'll have to tell her what happened, and she'll probably blame me for letting Roddy go near the lake by himself."

Rosemary had a bright idea. "I know! We'll go home to my house and clean him up there."

"Oh, would you mind doing that, Rosemary? Thanks a lot. I shan't mind telling Mum about the swan if Roddy is returned clean!"

"We'd better go, then," said Rosemary.

"What about your Nature-study? That's what you were coming to the park for, isn't it?"

"It'll keep. Gaining a badge isn't all that important. It's interesting to work for a badge, but it's only a small part of Guiding."

"You sometimes make me want to join Guides," admitted Mandy. "I don't think I should ever be like you, though; I'm not an efficient sort of person."

Rosemary laughed. "It takes all sorts to make up Guiding, you know! Guides are only ordinary girls. Guide training is good, though; it helps you a lot in all kinds of unexpected ways."

Once again Roddy had pedalled away in advance of the girls. Mandy called anxiously to him.

"Come back, Roddy! You must stay with us."

"Shan't!" Roddy yelled back.

Mandy turned despairingly to Rosemary. "What can anybody do with him, Rosemary?"

"Could I try something with him, Mandy? I gained the Child Nurse badge last year, and I learned a lot working for it."

"If you can do anything with Roddy, you're welcome to try."

Rosemary was fond of children. She knew what a big part make-believe plays in their lives. She called after Roddy.

"You're going to guard the princess, aren't you, Roddy? If you're not by her carriage, the enemy may carry her off."

Roddy stopped abuptly. Then, to Mandy's astonishment, he turned his tricycle round and rode back to them. The baby has suddenly been transformed into a princess and he into a brave soldier guarding it. It did the trick!

On the way home, Mandy learned a number of things about managing a child. Instead of rushing on to the zebra crossing, Roddy was prevailed upon by Rosemary to pause. Rosemary said, "Will you make sure it's safe for the princess to cross the river, Roddy?"

"I'll just see if it's safe," replied Roddy, and looked closely both ways before setting off across the zebra.

"You've certainly got the knack of catching Roddy's

interest," Mandy said admiringly. "I'll have to try this kind of thing next time I take him for a walk."

"A bit of imagination goes a long way in dealing with children," said Rosemary.

"All the same, I know now why you're a Patrol Leader, Rosemary."

Mandy was deeply impressed by Rosemary's handling of two situations, one dangerous and one difficult.

"You know, Rosemary, I'd like to try Guides. I could do with a spot of—well, training. I'd like to be efficient, like you, and able to take care of things that crop up."

"Well, don't imagine that Guides will turn you into a kind of supergirl! Guiding is fun, though, and I'd love you to come into the Robin Patrol."

At Rosemary's house Roddy received a much-needed wash and brush-up, which he suffered without too much fuss on the strength of a promise of cakes and lemonade afterwards!

"Thanks a lot, Rosemary," said Mandy, as Roddy led the way out of Rosemary's house. "I've learnt something today, thanks to you."

"Bang, bang!" shouted Roddy. "I is shootin' down the enemy that's trying to capture the princess!"

"See you at Guides, Mandy," said Rosemary softly, and closed the door.

P.L. OF THE TIGER PATROL

"I was in the Pixies in Brownies," said Angela. "Now I'm in the Tigers in Guides. It's a funny name for a Guide Patrol, isn't it, Mrs. Blake?"

Mrs. Blake, the Guider of the 1st Northam Guide Company, laughed.

"Yes. Most Guide Patrols take the name of a bird or a flower, though some Patrols nowadays call themselves after famous men or women, or take even quite way-out names. But there's a special reason for the Tiger Patrol's name, Angela. Your Patrol Leader, Georgina, will tell you and the other new Guides in the Patrol about it."

Angela nodded and hurried away to join her new Patrol and hear how they got the—for Guides—unusual name of the Tigers.

This, filled out and elaborated, is the story Georgina, the Patrol Leader, told.

Caroline and Suzanne lived in the same village, Stratton, and were both in the Nightingale Patrol of the 1st Northam Company. Caroline was P.L.

Stratton was some distance by road from the Guide hall at Northam, but there was a short cut through the woods of Lord Stratton's large deer-park, and this the girls took on the evenings the Guide Company met.

On leaving the Guide hall one evening in summer, the two girls followed their usual route over a meadow to one of the stiles leading into Stratton Park. Just as Suzanne mounted the stile, however, a tall, lean man dressed in a leather jacket and breeches hurried from the undergrowth and gestured Suzanne back.

"Sorry, missy, but you can't come through the woods," he said. "Not today. There's trouble with the deer. They could be dangerous. Please keep out."

"Oh!" said Suzanne, in surprise, dropping back.

"I didn't know deer could be dangerous," said Caroline. "I always thought deer were timid."

"The stags get fierce at certain times of the year—and this is one of 'em."

"But we always go through the park to Stratton," protested Caroline. "We came through on our way to Guides only a couple of hours ago."

"You'll be able to use the park again after today," the man assured her. "Just for now please go another way to Stratton."

"Very well." Reluctantly, Suzanne turned from the stile, and after a moment's hesitation Caroline followed her.

"Thank you," the man called after them, as they walked away.

"Well, we've got a nice long walk in front of us now," remarked Suzanne.

"Long but not so nice," commented Caroline. "It's just beginning to rain."

Neither girl had brought a raincoat, as the weather had been fine when they left home. Now the rain began to fall heavily.

"We'd better shelter," said Suzanne, and ran for the trees overhanging the meadow from the woods.

"You know," said Caroline, "I'm a bit puzzled by that man. He looked like a gamekeeper, but I've never seen him before. He was quite polite and all that, but I'm wondering if he isn't a poacher."

"A poacher?"

"He might be after the deer! I've heard that there's quite a bit of deer-poaching going on in private estates. Deer fetch money as meat—venison, in fact. You remember Robin Hood and his Merry Men practically lived on venison in Sherwood Forest. I'm sure they wouldn't have stayed merry if Friar Tuck hadn't brought along a trout or two to eat as a change."

"How you do burble on!" said Suzanne. "What's Robin Hood's diet got to do with being caught in heavy rain and banned from our short cut through Stratton Woods?"

"Like I said, ducky—poaching deer. Suppose that man is after bagging a brace of deer—with accomplices, no doubt. What would he do when he saw two uniformed figures—us, my dear—about to enter the deer-park? He'd at once hatch up a way to keep us out. So he spins a yarn about deer being dangerous."

"Stags! I've heard that stags do turn nasty at certain periods of the year. They shed their antlers or something."

"I can't see anything dangerous about a stag with its antlers shed. It would be a sight more dangerous with 'em on."

"They may be fierce at the same time as they shed

their antlers," admitted Suzanne, "but—oh, dear, I don't really know."

"There's one thing I know," said Caroline briskly. "I'm not going to get soaking wet by trudging through heavy rain for a couple of miles when we can get home in next to no time and keep dry in the process by going through the woods, stags or no stags. Come on, Sue—follow your Leader!"

"You're not! Oh, Caroline, d'you think we ought—after what that man said?"

"I do and I'm going to. Come on!"

Suiting the action to the word, Caroline clambered up the stone wall enclosing Stratton Park. Suzanne followed slowly. She was more formal and less bold than Caroline, who was robust, energetic and adventurous. Caroline helped her over the wall, and then the two stepped through the undergrowth to join the track that led to Stratton. Suzanne, despite Caroline's bold steps, trod warily even when she reached the track, and she cast anxious eyes into the thick bushes that bordered the track.

But it was Caroline who came to a sudden, startled halt. As she did so, she turned and gripped Suzanne's arm, at the same time putting her fingers to her lips.

"Look—over there!" she breathed. "Just as I said, they're poachers—laying snares or something."

Following her gaze, Suzanne caught a glimpse through the undergrowth of a man crouching down with a big net in his hands. He appeared to be young and long-haired, but the girls didn't pause to scrutinize him. They sank back into concealment in the undergrowth alongside the path.

"They're going to net deer," Caroline breathed into Suzanne's ear. "We've got to stop 'em, Sue."

"H—h—how?" asked Suzanne, who was shivering slightly with fright.

"We've got to get to the gamekeeper's house, and tell him. Listen, Sue! I'm going to sneak through the vegetation till I'm out of sight of the poacher. You follow me. We've both done tracking and stalking in Guides, so now's our chance to put it to real use."

Suzanne nodded.

Slowly and with extreme caution, Caroline crawled through the vegetation. She intended to reach a point where she would be completely out of sight of the poacher, then take a roundabout course until she struck the track again. Once there, she and Suzanne could race to the gamekeeper's cottage and raise the alarm.

Suzanne, fearful of being left alone, squirmed swiftly through the undergrowth to get alongside Caroline, and then, side by side, the two girls crawled as fast as they dared towards the point that Caroline estimated would take them outside the poacher's range of vision.

But they didn't reach their objective.

Raising her head cautiously above the vegetation to see how far off they were, Caroline suddenly froze. Her face drained to a ghostly whiteness. Her hand reached out to grip Suzanne's, but it was nerveless and slid down as it touched Suzanne.

In the same instant Suzanne saw, and almost fainted.

A few yards away, flat in the undergrowth, lay a full-grown tiger.

It had been fast asleep, but now it was disturbed. It opened its eyes, looked up, and saw the girls.

The next moment was the most terrifying the two Guides ever experienced.

For a second, in utter silence, the girls stared at the tiger, and the tiger stared at them. Then, giving a prodigious yawn, the tiger rose, stretched itself, and stalked disdainfully away, as much as to say: "Well, now you've disturbed my rest with your silly stalking game I'd better go and find somewhere else to sleep."

Caroline and Suzanne simply collapsed. They stayed where they were for some seconds, utterly overcome by the startling, flabbergasting encounter and too scared to move.

It was only when a sudden shout came from somewhere not far away that they jumped up.

"He's here! Ajax, Ajax! Got 'im! Give us a hand here quick, Palo!"

Gazing in the direction of the sound, the girls saw the man who had kept them out of the woods struggling with a great net, in which the tiger appeared to be enmeshed. He was yelling for "Palo", who soon came running through the vegetation to lend a hand. Palo, the Guides noticed, was the young, long-haired man they had first seen with the net.

"I see it all now," said Caroline, "or most of it. That man kept us out of the woods because he knew the tiger was here. Gosh, Sue, it doesn't bear thinking about what might have happened to us."

"L—let's go," urged Suzanne, her voice trembling. "I don't want to stay here another minute."

As they moved along the track, however, the tall,

lean man saw them. He came running over to them.

"You know! You saw!" he said. "You shouldn't have come in. Ajax is not fierce, but he might have hurt you. He is in the net now. I must go and get the truck round for him. Please, young ladies, I beg you not to tell that there was a tiger loose. It could do me harm. The tiger is very valuable. I knew Palo and I could capture it if left alone. We could not bear to shoot him."

"Oh, no!" cried Caroline. "Not shoot it."

"That is what would have happened if it had become known. It would have been a heavy loss to me and my circus. Would you young ladies like to see the circus? Then come and ask for me and you shall have two of the best seats." He pulled a card from his pocket and thrust it into Caroline's hand. "I must go now. Please keep this to yourselves. I beg it of you. Thank you!"

With that he turned away.

Caroline wanted to stay to see the tiger again, but Suzanne insisted on going, so Caroline reluctantly went with her.

"But we will see the tiger again," she said gleefully —"at the circus!"

And they did.

That was the story Georgina told the new Guides, who had listened entranced and thrilled. Georgina had heard the story herself from a previous Patrol Leader, for it was a tradition in the Tiger Patrol that the P.L. should tell it to each intake of new Guides.

"After that adventure the Nightingale Patrol voted unanimously to change their name to the Tiger Patrol. Of course, it happened a long time ago, as you can tell."

"I don't see how we can tell." Angela spoke up. "It could have happened quite a short time ago, couldn't it?"

Georgina gestured towards the Guider, Mrs. Blake. "She's very old, you know. It happened when she was P.L. of the Nightingales, ages ago. She's Caroline Blake."

THE PATROL THAT CHANGED ITS NAME

"It's a pity B.–P. didn't have Stormy to advise him when he founded Guides," said Gillian. "Things would have been a lot different today."

"A lot," agreed Sarah. "There wouldn't be any Guides left!"

The other Guides in the 4th Beckwith Company's H.Q. hut laughed.

"All the same," put in Laura, P.L. of the Owls, "you've got to admit that Stormy's alive!"

"Alive and kicking," agreed Mary, her Second—"but kicking too much!"

That about summed up the general opinion in the Company of Storm Harrison, who was the newest member of the Owl Patrol. Storm was well nicknamed "Stormy". Storm by name, she was stormy by nature. Quick and imaginative, she was also restless and critical, impatient of anyone or anything that seemed "stick-in-the-muddish". One of the Owl Patrol's complaints against her was that she was always wanting to change things. She hadn't been a Guide five minutes before she expressed the opinion that what the Guides needed was a complete change of uniform, "something really eye-catching and up to the minute". She soon made it known that several of the tests for badges were in dire need of revision or replacement, and all the badges needed brightening up. But it was her latest suggestion for reform that set the Owl Patrol by the ears. This was no less than that the Owls should change their name!

"Every blessed Patrol is the Owls or the Robins or the Kingfishers," she complained. "Why can't we be *different*? Why can't we take the name of an uncommon bird?"

"Because," explained Laura. "B.–P. advised Scouts and Guides to adopt an animal or bird for their Patrol emblem that they really could study, as you will discover if you read *Scouting for Boys* carefully. It would be silly to call ourselves the Albatross Patrol when we haven't the faintest chance of studying the albatross."

"What Patrol would you suggest we become, Stormy," asked Gillian—"the Dodo Patrol?"

"It wouldn't be out of place," retorted Stormy. "Some of you are almost extinct!"

The Guides yelled with laughter, as much at Gillian's furious face as at the sally.

But Stormy was serious and persistent. "We could be the Eagle Patrol. There are eagles in the Scottish mountains, and Northumberland isn't so far from Scotland. Eagles sound really exciting, and we could study them through books and pictures, even if we didn't actually see one."

Something of Stormy's keenness and enthusiasm did infect one or two members of the Patrol. Sally and Anne spoke up in support of the suggestion, but in the eyes of the others Stormy was a malcontent and not stable enough to inspire confidence. They vetoed her notions.

"What a lot of stick-in-the-muds you are!" complained Stormy, but without malice. "Whatever you

115

say, it would be wizard to be Eagles instead of stuffy old Owls."

The Company's Easter camp was only a few days away, and gave Stormy's imagination something to feed on till the time came for her to go.

The camp was sited in a picturesque and mountainous part of Northumberland. The country was wild and lonely, but in one corner of it the Government had built a large radar missile detection and defence station of a "top secret" character. This had brought forth violent protests from the public both on the score of its cost and its situation in one of the most beautiful parts of Northumberland, but it had arisen despite these and now stood, ringed by a high electrified wire fence, in the shadow of silent mountains, craggy grey peaks and rolling heather moors. It could not be seen from the Guides' camp, which lay on the foothills between two mountains, but Stormy became aware of it in an exciting—and dangerous—way.

Tracking competitions between Patrols were among the popular events organised at the camp. Stormy and Anne were chosen to lay a trail up the Black Mountain and evade capture by the several Patrols following them. They set off soon after breakfast, carrying their lunch in rucksacks. They climbed the silent, shadowy pass that gashed the stony heart of the Black Mountain, came out into the warm sunshine of a high heathery plateau, ate their lunch beside a swift, foaming mountain beck—and suddenly found the landscape fading before their eyes. Almost before they realised what was happening they were blanketed in a dense, damp, grey mist that shut out sight and sound in the space of minutes. It was quite a frightening experience for Anne, but Stormy revelled in it.

"Gosh, Anne!" she said excitedly. "I've read about people being trapped on mountains in mist, but I never thought I'd be in one."

Anne shivered. "It's horrible. Supposing it doesn't lift, Stormy?"

"We won't wait for it to lift," replied Stormy cheerfully. "We'll go on down. It's probably only lying on the top of the mountain. We'll soon get out of it."

"But we can't see a yard in front of us!" Anne's voice was quite horror-stricken. "We might walk over a precipice."

"If you don't know what's what you easily might, but I happen to know what to do. We can't go wrong if we follow the stream."

"Follow the stream?"

"Yes. We're lucky; we've got a stream right at our feet. It's bound to lead us into the valley. It's as good as a road—better! Come on! Keep close together, so that we shan't lose each other."

"Wait a minute!" said Anne, grabbing Stormy's arm. "Wouldn't it be better to stay where we are? We've left signs for the others to track us by. They're bound to find us if we stay put."

"Always supposing the mist lifts. But what if it doesn't? It may lie on this mountain plateau for hours. If you fancy spending the night up here, I don't!"

Anne hesitated. Then, reluctantly, she followed as Stormy moved off.

It was easy to keep to the course of the stream,

which was noisy enough to guide them by sound alone, but to Anne at least the journey was a nightmare. She could only just make out the blurred, ghostly form of Stormy in front, and they were too occupied on keeping their feet to talk. Hummocks of grass made them stumble, unsuspected boulders cut and bruised them. and the dank, cloying mist chilled and blinded them.

For what seemed to Anne mile after mile they trudged down alongside the chattering stream. For most of the way Stormy was in front, but presently her shoelace came undone and she stopped.

"Don't go too far, Anne," she called, as Anne passed her. "We don't want to get parted."

"We shan't if we follow the stream—remember?" replied Anne, rather acidly. She was feeling out of humour and dejected. What had promised to be a most enjoyable outing had turned into an uncomfortable, not to say risky, experience.

"Cheer up!" Stormy called after her—then added sharply, "My goodness!" and sprang to her feet in alarm. As she had bent down to tie up her lace she realised that the stream had ceased to chatter, that another sound had replaced the sing-song of the swift, eddying water.

The new sound was the swish of water falling into space.

Galvanised into rapid action by a dreadful fear, she leapt forward and grabbed frantically at Anne, pulling her to a standstill.

"Anne, stop!" she shouted. "I believe the stream——!"

She didn't finish, for at that moment, with the

suddenness of a transformation scene in a pantomime, the sun broke through the mist. Like curtains parting, the grey vapour rolled slowly away in front and on either side of them, and their horrified eyes beheld the cliff dropping sheer away down into the valley three hundred feet or more below, the stream spraying its waters out down the cliff-face in a series of rivulets.

Anne's face turned chalk-white as she saw the edge of the precipice yawning not more than three feet distant from her.

"M-my stars, Stormy!" she whispered. "We—I nearly went over!"

Stormy nodded dumbly. She couldn't speak. Limply, she sank down in the heather.

"Another foot or two——" Anne stopped, shuddered, and dropped down beside Stormy.

"I blame that theory about following a stream—it's goofy," admitted Stormy.

"It is!" said Anne, with feeling. "If you hadn't grabbed me, Stormy, I'd have gone over."

"If my shoelace hadn't come undone I'd have gone over first."

"Have you any idea where we are?"

"Not a clue. I only hope we're not far from camp, that's all. I'm starving."

"I'm starving and all in as well."

"I'll go and have a peek over that line of boulders over there. Coming?"

"I couldn't even crawl there. Oh, well, yes, I'd better."

A tumbled row of boulders to the right of them shut
119

off the panorama beyond from their view. Crossing the stream, they made their way across the boulders. The mist had almost entirely cleared now, and the valley lay outspread below in sunlight. But the two Guides had no eyes for the beauty of the landscape. Almost, it seemed, within throwing distance of the clifftop stood a far-flung range of buildings, some curiously shaped, and ringed as far as the eye could see by a high fence.

"My goodness!" breathed Stormy. "That must be that new secret radar station."

"It can't be very secret, though, can it? It must cover dozens of acres!"

"Fancy striking it like this! We must somehow have come right over to the far side of Black Mountain. I'd no idea—Great Scott!"

"What's up?" demanded Anne.

But Stormy didn't answer till she had dragged Anne down behind one of the great boulders. "Didn't you see?" she whispered. "There are men—on the lower ridge from us. I saw two of them. What d'you think they're doing, Anne?" Stormy dropped her voice still lower. "They're spying on the radar station!"

Anne stared at her. "Spying?" she repeated sceptically.

"Look for yourself. But keep your head down. They're looking at the radar station through a telescope."

Unbelievingly, Anne peered round the boulder in the direction Stormy had indicated. Then she caught her breath. "By gosh, you're right!" she breathed. "They haven't seen us, or heard us, Stormy. They'd better not do, either, or we'll be in trouble. I think the other man's got a camera, photographing the radar station. What had we better do?"

"Get back to camp as fast as we can and report it. They must be spies. Men don't keep a watch on a top-secret radar establishment through a telescope for fun."

Anne nodded. "Come on!"

But getting back to camp was not so easy, especially as they reasoned it might be unwise to go near to the cliff-top watchers to risk making their presence known. In the end the two Guides decided there was only one safe course left open to them. That was to follow the stream back up to the plateau from whence they had descended in the mist and find their way back to camp by their own tracking signs.

It was more than two hours later that, dusty, dishevelled and utterly weary, the two Guides were hailed by a party led by their own P.L., Laura Drake, who had been systematically searching the tracks on either side of the main pass.

"Thank goodness we've found you," said Laura, in deep relief. "All the camp's been out after you. Badger's been desperately worried. She's even sent to Thraxton for the mountain-rescue team to come up."

"We lost track of you at the top of the pass," said Gillian.

"What happened to you?" demanded Mary.

Stormy cast a warning glance at Anne "We got lost in the mist," she said briefly. "We'll tell you all about it when we've fed and rested. At the moment we're on our last legs and ready to turn cannibal. Let's keep moving."

"Anne will bear me out, Badger. We saw two men spying on the radar station from the cliff."

"Are you sure they were spying?" asked the Guider doubtfully. "They could have been admiring the view, you know."

"What through a telescope, Badger?" asked Anne.

"They were photographing it, too," added Stormy.

"It does sound odd," admitted the Guider. She didn't say so, but she was thinking of Stormy's well-known tendency towards flights of fancy. Anne was different, but Badger reasoned that she might have had her imagination excited by Stormy. "One must be wary of putting some sinister interpretation on what could be a perfectly harmless occupation."

Further discussion was interrupted by the entry into the tent of the Assistant Guider, who came to announce the arrival of the mountain-rescue team from Thraxton.

"Supposing you tell the leader of the mountain-rescue team what you saw," Badger suggested to Stormy and Anne, before hurrying out to greet the team of four and explain to them that the "lost" Guides had returned safely.

Stormy nodded glumly. "I suppose he'll laugh at us," she confided to Anne. "It's obvious Badger thinks we're romancing, so I expect the mountain-climbers will, too."

The mountain-rescue team leader, James Gavin, did not laugh outright when the Guides told him of the suspicious activities of the two men with the telescope, but the lines of amusement that crinkled his leathery mouth left Stormy and Anne in no doubt that he disbelieved in "spies".

"It's hard to see quite what information of any value they could get from watching the radar station," he said, "but I don't know anything about these things. I tell you what I'll do, though—when I get back to Thraxton I'll tell Detective-Sergeant Connell about it. It's more in his line than mine. He belongs to the mountain-rescue team, and would have been with us this evening if he hadn't had to stay on urgent duty. How'll that do?"

"It'll give somebody else a laugh, at any rate," Stormy muttered crossly to Anne, as Mr. Gavin and his companions took their leave. "After this, a boulder can fall on the radar-station, for all I care."

"Perhaps that's what the men have got in mind——" suggested Anne, "pushing boulders over on to it."

"Don't you start being funny about it!" protested Stormy indignantly.

Vexed and glum at the sceptical reception accorded their exciting news of spies on the Black Mountain, Stormy and Anne retired to the privacy of their own tent and turned in early. Both were tired and slept soundly. Next morning after breakfast they received an urgent call to Badger's tent, where, to their surprise, they were introduced to Detective-Sergeant Connell and two other men, who, he explained, were not policemen but rock-climbers and members of the local mountain vigilante group.

"I've called to investigate something you told James Gavin last evening, missy," Detective-Sergeant Connell said to Stormy. "It was too late to do anything about it last night, but we've come along first thing this morning to ask if you could guide us up to the place where you saw these two men with a telescope.

Your Guider has kindly agreed to let you go if the Assistant Guider accompanies you, and we'd be most obliged if you could start at once, if you're willing to show us the way."

"Are they spies, then?" asked Stormy excitedly.

"We're not sure what they are yet, miss," Detective-Sergeant Connell told her, "but we've got our suspicions. Saboteurs might be a better word."

"I said they might want to push boulders down on to the radar-station!" cried Anne.

The Guides were soon climbing with the Assistant-Guider, camp-named Antelope, and the three men up the pass they had ascended the previous day.

"What I'm chiefly afraid of," Detective-Sergeant Connell confided to them, "is that we may be too late."

"Why should we be?" inquired Anne curiously.

"Because they may have got what they came for—and gone," replied the detective-sergeant. "I'd have started out last night, as soon as James Gavin told me what you'd seen, but it would have been dark before we could begin climbing, so I had to wait till this morning."

The two men with Detective-Sergeant Connell spoke hardly at all throughout the entire journey. Connell, on the few occasions he addressed them, called them Bill and Greg.

"The strong, silent type, evidently," Stormy confided to Anne, who giggled.

"From now on," Detective-Sergeant Connell warned the Guides when Stormy pointed out that they were nearing the cliff-face over which the stream fell, "be as quiet as you possibly can. We've got to spring

124

a surprise on those men. If they're there and they hear us they'll bolt."

For the first time Bill spoke. He nodded at the Guides. "They'd best keep well away in case there's trouble, Jim," he said to Connell.

Stormy turned swiftly on him. "If you're going to try and keep us out of the best bit we jolly well won't show you the way any further!"

"We must do whatever is wise, Stormy," Antelope put in.

Connell grinned. "I'm sure it'll be all right, ma'am. We'll be able to handle anything that's going." To Stormy: "Lead on, Girl Guide!"

Stormy cast a stern glance on Bill and then pointed to the row of boulders outlined mistily against the skyline. "Those are the boulders we saw them from."

"Come on, then—and keep your heads down!"

Swiftly and silently, he and his two companions ran towards the line of boulders. Stooping low, the Guides and Antelope kept up with them, until, within a few yards of the cliff edge, Connell signalled to Stormy and Anne to lead the way to the point from which they had watched the "spies". The Guides did so. Then, taking care not to expose themselves, they peered out towards the lower ridge on which, yesterday, they had seen the two men with the telescope. Then Stormy let out a gasp.

"Look!" she breathed out to Detective-Sergeant Connell, who had crawled up behind her. "There's one of them!"

"And the other's on the end of a rope!" exclaimed Connell. "We've caught 'em red-handed, by George!"

Calling to Bill and Greg, he cast aside all attempt at concealment and made his way, running and leaping, towards the lower ridge.

The man who, Stormy and Anne could see now, was paying out a rope down the cliff, heard him coming and shouted a warning to his unseen companion below. Without letting go of the rope that was supporting the other he could do nothing to escape, and within a few minutes he was in the grasp of Detective-Sergeant Connell. Bill and Greg took over his rope and proceeded to haul the man on the end of it back up to the clifftop.

"It's all right, there's no danger," Connell called to the two Guides, who had been left well behind by the sudden dash of the three men. "And we're in time, thanks to you two!"

"But—but—I don't understand!" exclaimed Stormy, and gazed in perplexity as a big man with a face dark with frustration and fury appeared over the lip of the cliff and was promptly secured by Bill and Greg.

"Egg-thieves," Connell explained, with great satisfaction. "I suspected it when Gavin told me what you'd seen. Gavin's only interested in rock-climbing and mountain rescue. I and Bill and Greg are interested in the birds that nest in the mountains, especially eagles."

"Eagles?" exclaimed Stormy and Anne together.

Antelope gazed inquiringly at Connell.

"Yes, eagles! Those are what these two beauties are after—or, at least, their eggs. A pair were reported as having been seen in Northumberland—the first for years and years. These clever dicks have found their eyrie, which is more than we did, and they were going to raid the nest. They weren't wasting any time about it, either. How much would the eggs bring you, eh?" he asked the roped man. "Two hundred pounds each, I dare bet. Worth taking a spot of risk for, I must admit. Well, eagles are protected birds, so I'm charging you both under the Act. I only hope to goodness you haven't scared them away."

Fortunately, the detective-sergeant and his companions had arrived before the egg-thief had descended near enough to the eyrie to alarm the eagles.

"But if it hadn't been for you two this might have been the first and last time we'd have had eagles nesting in the Black Mountain—or in Northumberland," Connell told Stormy and Anne gratefully. "And now that we've had the eyrie located for us we'll take good care that nobody goes near it or disturbs it. That's why we didn't tell you or your Guiders about the eagles. We didn't—and don't—want a crowd of sightseers peering at them—so we'll get you all to keep the situation of it to yourselves."

"We'll do that," agreed Antelope, "and I'm sure you can rely on the Guides to keep it secret."

"We'll keep mum," promised Anne.

"Provided we can tell the Patrol that there *are* eagles!" added Stormy.

Connell laughed. "There's no objection to that!"

"To think it wasn't the radar-station those men were spying on!" remarked Anne to Stormy, as they wended their way down the pass behind Connell and his captives—"only eagles!"

"*Only* eagles!" echoed Stormy. "Eagles are a jolly sight more interesting than a blessed radar-station. I reckon after this, Anne, we'll have a strong case for calling ourselves the Eagle Patrol!"

In that opinion Stormy found she had the whole-hearted support of the entire Owl Patrol—and Badger, who said that whilst Guides didn't expect rewards for their good turns this was a reward that was completely proper and fitting.

So, on the last night of camp, round a glowing camp-fire, the Owl Patrol, with impressive symbolism and ceremony, took its new name of the Eagle Patrol.